'It's best to make your position clear

from the beginning,' Philip replied, keeping his tone light and casual. 'Friendship is rare between men and women, but it can be very rewarding. Do you agree?'

'Oh, yes, certainly,' Megan said, her tone and expression giving nothing away. 'As long as the position is clear from the start, no one gets hurt.'

'That's what I've always thought,' Philip said. 'I hope we'll be good friends, Megan.'

'I see no reason why we shouldn't be...'

Anne Herries lives in Cambridge but spends part of the winter in Spain, where she and her husband stay in a pretty resort nestled amid the hills that run from Malaga to Gibraltar. Gazing over a sparkling blue ocean, watching the sunbeams dance like silver confetti on the restless waves, Anne loves to dream up her stories of laughter, tears and romantic lovers. She is the author of over thirty published novels, many of them for Harlequin Mills & Boon. Writing has been a dream come true—a dream she enjoys sharing with her readers.

THE MOST PRECIOUS GIFT

BY
ANNE HERRIES

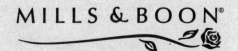

MILLS & BOON®

First published in Great Britain 2000
Harlequin Mills & Boon Limited,
Eton House, 18-24 Paradise Road, Richmond, Surrey TW9 1SR

© Anne Herries 2000

ISBN 0 263 82259 1

Set in Times Roman 10½ on 12 pt.
03-0009-50858

Printed and bound in Spain
by Litografia Rosés, S.A., Barcelona

CHAPTER ONE

DR PHILIP GRANT waited patiently for the large, expensive car to discharge its passenger, before driving into his parking space in the grounds of the cottage hospital. He knew the other driver well, a local and very wealthy farmer, but he had no idea of the woman's identity. However, as she got out of the car, he had plenty of time to admire the view.

Whoever she was, she had gorgeous legs! And a figure to match if he wasn't mistaken.

She was wearing a long, belted, camel coat, but even the bulky material couldn't make her look anything other than elegant. She had poise, and as she turned her head his way he had time to notice that she was beautiful— blonde hair, green eyes and a face that seemed in some way familiar.

Briefly, he was puzzled as for an instant he thought he might know her from somewhere, but she turned her head away too soon for him to be able to recognise her. He frowned as the memory eluded him. As she walked away, he saw that he could now safely park in his allotted space, and did so. By the time he had finished manoeuvring, she had disappeared inside the hospital.

As Philip got out of his car, Robert Crawley wound the window down on his BMW and called to him.

'Sorry if I held you up, Dr Grant. I was just delivering Sister Hastings. She doesn't actually start until tomorrow, but she wanted to have a look around this afternoon. Get a feel for the place, if you see what I mean.'

'Oh, yes. I'd forgotten we were getting a replacement for Sister Marsh this week. It was very kind of you to bring her over, Crawley.'

'She's without a car at the moment, so she asked me if I'd oblige. As it happens, she's a friend of my sister. They knew each other years ago apparently. Olive asked me to look out for her and, after meeting her, I can tell you that won't be a problem at all.' Crawley grinned his appreciation of the woman who had just left his car.

'Sister Hastings…' Philip frowned as he struggled to recall something and failed. The name seemed to ring a bell but he couldn't think why. He shook his head, turning to more important things. 'Are you coming to the hospital's darts match on Friday, Crawley? All the money we raise will be for the new children's unit.'

'Sorry, can't make it. I have a meeting,' Robert Crawley replied. 'But you know you can count on me for a cheque. Always glad to help the Chestnuts.' He arched his brows at Philip. 'Not playing yourself, I understand?'

'Not my game. I prefer squash—or skiing when I can find the time to get away,' Philip replied. He *had* been asked to join the village darts team, but his leisure time was precious and he used it judiciously. 'As you know, the fixture has been a regular event for years, but this year, as chairman of the children's fund, I decided to hijack it for the cause. All the players have to be sponsored for as much as possible—and then we're going to have the one-hundred-and-eighty competition. All entrants are required to pay five pounds. I dare say I shall have a go at that.'

'They will expect you to,' Crawley replied. 'Have to please the lesser mortals, Doctor. I dare say they think it's quite a feather in their caps to have got you involved.'

'Oh, I doubt I've made that much difference. Lady Rowen twisted my arm a little, but that's her way.' He smiled at the other man. 'Thank you for the offer of a cheque, Crawley. I know you've been generous to us in the past. You must come to Susan's for a drink before Christmas. I'll ask her to arrange it.'

'Always pleased to see your sister. I must go now, and so must you. I'm sure you're busy.'

Philip nodded, pressed the electronic key on his eighteen-month-old Golf and made his way into the hospital. Visiting the wards where his patients were recovering from operations carried out at Addenbrookes, the excellent Cambridge hospital, was one of Philip's favourite duties. As an overworked GP, who spent much of his spare time attending meetings organised for the benefit of patients and villagers, he still found time to check on his convalescing patients at least once a week.

This particular afternoon, he was planning to visit a young girl who was a favourite of his. Jennifer Russell had been in and out of hospital for much of her young life. She had been born with a slight deformity of the spine, as well as club-foot—talipes calcaneus—which meant she could walk only on the heel of her left foot. This latest operation, the last of several, had been meant to help her walk more easily. She had been doing well on his last visit, listening to her physiotherapist and working hard. He knew she was hoping he was going to allow her home this afternoon.

He went first to the men's post-operative ward, stopping to chat to an elderly patient who was recovering from a proctocolectomy—surgical removal of the colon and rectum. It was a dramatic procedure for many patients, and the resulting changes to their lives were often difficult to accept. Philip knew Mr Jarvis was very depressed about the whole thing and would need help to come to terms with what had happened.

He spent half an hour sitting on the man's bed, talking him through various aspects of his condition that bothered him, then walked down the corridor to the children's ward. He could hear laughter as he approached, and smiled. It always amazed Philip how brave the children were. No matter how serious their illnesses, they seemed to have so much courage in facing up to whatever happened.

Jennifer was no exception. Philip had visited her in hospital many times over the years, and knew what to expect. She was sitting on the edge of her bed, her legs dangling, while one of the junior nurses painted her toenails.

The children's ward was painted in bright colours, with murals on the walls, a TV in one corner and a pile of books and toys at the far end. At the moment there were two other children there, apart from Jennifer, both of whom seemed to be busy, reading.

'Dr Grant.' Jennifer smiled as she saw him, and wriggled her toes. 'Don't you think I'm posh today? Sister Hastings says this colour is all the rage now.'

Philip hadn't immediately noticed the woman standing quietly near his patient. She appeared to have been looking out at the pleasant grounds, which were white with frost this particular afternoon, but turned as her name was mentioned, a smile on her lips.

'It's called Redheaded Momma,' she said, and smiled, a hint of mischief in her voice. 'Very daring. I bought some myself when I was in London.'

It was that wicked smile that suddenly brought the

memories flooding back. Of course! No wonder she looked familiar. He should have known her at once. She'd changed a lot, though. When he'd last seen her, she'd been a bubbly, fun-loving, eighteen-year-old student with long hair—and about a stone heavier in weight.

Megan Hastings! The young girl he'd parted from just a few months before he'd met Helen...

He wondered if she would remember him, but it had been a long time ago and they'd both changed. They'd been very young and a little naïve that summer, both caught up in their own worlds—and they hadn't exactly parted on good terms, though he couldn't recall exactly why.

'Sister Hastings?' Philip smiled and walked over to her, extending his hand. 'I'm Philip Grant. I have a surgery in the village. I've just popped in to have a look at Jennifer.'

'Hello. I'm not officially on duty yet,' she replied, accepting his hand. Hers felt cool and slender, and was soon removed from his firm grasp. Obviously, she wanted to keep her distance. 'I've been told about you but, of course, we've met before.'

'Yes...I wondered if you'd remember.' Philip gave her a rueful look. 'It's been a long time....'

'Yes, it must be ten years,' she said. 'I was a student nurse when you were a junior houseman at Guy's. We only went out together a couple of times...'.

'More than that, I think,' he replied, a puzzled expression in his eyes. Why was she denying that they'd known each other pretty well for several months? Did he detect a slight hostility in her manner? 'I may be advancing in years, but I seem to remember you came along to the rugby field to support the medical students' team—and we went to concerts a few times.'

'In a crowd,' she said, and smiled oddly. 'Yes, I suppose if you think of it like that, we did.' Her manner indicated that she was ready to leave. He was puzzled, wondering what he'd done to displease her. She couldn't still be angry because of the way they'd parted. He seemed to remember some sort of an argument, but still couldn't recall the reason for their quarrel. 'It was nice meeting you, Dr Grant. I'm expected elsewhere in a few minutes. I'll leave you to talk to Jennifer.' She smiled warmly at the young girl. 'I'll come and see you again tomorrow—if you're still here. I might just have a lipstick to match that polish. Goodbye for now, Doctor.'

'I expect we'll meet another day,' Philip said, nodding and experiencing a slight feeling of regret. She was certainly lovely, and he had liked her smile.

He watched as she walked from the small ward. She'd left her coat somewhere and was wearing a slim-fitting grey skirt with a silk blouse of a slightly paler shade. Her blonde hair was cut in a neat style that was swept back and tucked behind her ears, and those long, long legs looked wonderful in black stockings and high heels. He imagined she wore more sensible shoes for work.

Philip brought his wandering thoughts back to the present with a jolt. What did it matter what Sister Hastings wore, on or off duty? His interest in women of late had been that of an observer only. Since his divorce, his few brief encounters with the opposite sex had been less than satisfactory.

'Can I go home?'

Jennifer's question made him give her his full attention. He examined her foot, though he knew the operation had been successful. She still had a foot that would never look or function quite normally, but it was very much better after the surgeon's work. She should, with a little practice, be able to wear a pair of special trainers instead of the built-up shoe she'd hated so much.

'Can I?' she asked anxiously. 'You said when I could walk from here to the door, without stopping, I could—and I can.'

'Show me,' he invited, smiling as she wriggled off the bed. Her walk was still awkward, still not as easy as he'd hoped, but a vast improvement on what it had been prior to the operation. 'Very good, Jennifer. You've been a good, brave girl—and I think you deserve a present.'

He opened his briefcase and took out the trainers he'd bought for her as a treat for all her hard work.

'For me?' She stared at him in delight, then threw her arms about his neck and hugged him. 'I do love you, Dr Philip!'

Philip laughed. Not many of his patients would have been bold enough to show their feelings as openly as this young girl. But Jenny had her own special charm, of which she was well aware and which she used quite blatantly at times. Philip found her refreshing, and was always uplifted by her wonderful courage.

His sister Susan sometimes told him that his manner with people outside his own circle of friends and family left something to be desired. 'You don't mean to be, Phil,' she'd told him, 'but you're rather intimidating at times. Though, of course, most people look up to doctors…so perhaps it isn't all your fault.'

Philip was quite unaware that he occasioned endless gossip amongst the nurses at the Chestnuts. Perhaps because he was so elusive. Living and working in the village, as he did, he was a part of the hospital and yet apart from it. And because he never asked out any of the hospital staff, a kind of legend had built up around him. Why wasn't he interested in women? They all refused to believe he might be gay, so there had to be some other explanation. Where did he spend his free time—and what had given him that aura of intrigue they all found so fascinating?

Had Philip known that he had that morning told Robert Crawley something many of the young nurses had been dying to find out, he would have been amused. He seldom spoke about his private life because there was no reason to do so—neither would he have been inclined to air his preferences on the hospital grapevine. He was, in fact, rather a private man.

Jennifer had slipped on her shoes and was admiring them. Philip smiled at her, pleased that he had thought to order them specially for her.

'You'll have to practise wearing them, but they have good support and shouldn't give you any pain. And now, young lady, I have work to do.'

He left the hospital, feeling pleased with his afternoon. Jennifer's mother, who was a close friend of his sister's, was coming to fetch her daughter that evening, and Mr Jarvis was feeling a little better now that they'd talked. It was on days like this that Philip really enjoyed being a doctor.

Sometimes, when he came to the end of a busy surgery then went home to his empty cottage, he felt helpless, knowing that there was so little he could do to help the patients who really needed him. It didn't matter how many times you had to deal with terminal cases, you never got really hardened to their distress. At least he hadn't, though he had acquired a calm, confident manner which usually reassured his patients.

Once upon a time, he had believed he could make a

difference. When he'd been very young and working at Guy's in London…

'Good grief!' he suddenly exclaimed as memory struck. He halted abruptly, clapping a hand to his forehead. 'She must think I'm an arrogant pig.'

Philip felt terrible as he remembered why he and Megan had stopped seeing each other. Megan had wanted him to go to a wedding with her, and he'd been playing in a squash tournament that weekend. He'd offered to go to the reception in the evening, but she'd suddenly put her foot down.

'No, that's not fair, Phil,' she'd cried, her face pink with annoyance. 'I've supported you week after week when you were playing rugby. Now when I ask you just once to do something for me, you won't.'

'Not won't—can't,' Philip had replied. 'Look, Megan, if it had been any other week…but I've promised…'

'All you ever think about is playing sport or going to the pub!'

Philip supposed her accusation had been fair at the time. As a student, he had joined most of the teams, both sporting and debating, because it had been expected of him. He and Megan had actually met in the pub all the students and young doctors had frequented. Philip had been a couple of years or so ahead of her in his training. He'd asked her out a few times on her own but, looking back, he realised she was right. They'd gone around in a crowd most of the time.

He'd assumed Megan had been happy with the arrangement. At that particular time of his life, Philip had had all the arrogance of youth. Working to pass his exams had taken so much of his energy and thought that perhaps he'd spared less for her than had been fair, expecting her to go along with his wishes because it had suited him.

He remembered now that he'd felt more upset than he'd expected when she'd told him she wasn't going to see him any more. He'd brooded over it for a few days, his feelings bruised, but then, when he'd made up his mind to apologise and ask her out somewhere nice, he'd discovered she'd disappeared from the scene. Her friend had told him she'd found a job somewhere else. He couldn't quite remember, but he thought she might have given him a phone number. He'd meant to call Megan, but his exams had become imminent and he'd forgotten.

After he'd passed his exams, life had seemed to speed up and open out for him. One of the changes had been that Helen had come into his world. Helen had been very different from the young nurses and medical students he'd met every day at the hospital. She had been Philip's own age, had come from a wealthy family and had run her own design business. They'd met, fallen in lust, married and divorced within five years.

He'd thought it had been love then, of course. Afterwards, he'd realised that it had been chemistry, nothing more and nothing less—good while it had lasted, but not deep enough to survive the test of time.

Helen had soon become disenchanted with being the wife of a struggling young doctor. She'd wanted much more than Philip could give her, and in the end she'd left him for a wealthy businessman.

By the time she'd left, Philip had been able to feel only relief. Any feelings they might have shared had been cancelled out by their frequent quarrels.

'Helen was too selfish,' Philip's sister had said afterwards. 'She could never understand your devotion to your patients. She wanted you to run after her like a little puppy dog. You're best away from her, Phil. You'll soon find someone new when your divorce comes through.'

But he hadn't. Since then, he'd avoided emotional entanglements. He wasn't still hankering after a lost love—it was more that he couldn't be bothered to try. He was too busy to risk getting entangled with another Helen. His work was too important.

He'd given up hospital work after the divorce, buying into a country practice a few miles from Susan and Mike. He enjoyed visiting them, and their two children. On the rare occasions he did date someone, it was usually for formal occasions. Susan usually fixed him up with one of her friends if he needed a partner. It was easier that way, and saved him having to chat them up. That made him a bit of a misogynist in some people's minds. He wasn't. He actually liked women, but relationships were too time-consuming. For a long time now he'd been too busy to think about his own feelings.

Philip was thoughtful as he drove back to the surgery through what was turning out to be a cold and murky afternoon. Susan had invited him over for dinner. He would ask her whom he should invite to Lady Rowen's New Year's Eve party…

The evening surgery had been heavier than normal. There had been the usual coughs and colds, a sprained ankle, a case of chronic indigestion which he thought needed further investigation, a couple of bad backs—genuine, he thought—and a child with suspected meningitis. He had sent mother and baby straight to the hospital, and would be telephoning later to discover whether his diagnosis had been correct. It wasn't always easy to be one hundred per cent sure with meningitis, but he never took chances with a child. It was better to be safe than sorry in his book.

Philip stopped at the small shop in the village, before driving to his sister's. He had run out of sugar that morning, and he disliked using the artificial stuff. While he was there he picked up an evening paper and a couple of comic books for the children.

The assistant liked to have a chat whenever he went in, and he listened patiently to her worries about her husband's bronchitis. Actually, Philip thought she probably suffered more than her husband did with her own arthritis, but she worried about his chest and it helped her to talk.

It was all of ten minutes before he was able to leave.

Philip was thoughtful as he drove to his sister's house. It was a sturdy, old-fashioned building with a large garden for the kids and five bedrooms—ideal for the extended family Susan had set her heart on. She already had one of each gender, but wanted at least four. Mike Blackwell, her adoring but long-suffering husband, often declared she was out to ruin him, but they were the happiest couple Philip knew.

Sometimes, when he saw them all together, he almost envied their happiness. He loved children, always had, but Helen had never wanted to be a mother. Maybe if they'd had a couple, she wouldn't have been so bored. Yet he knew in his heart he was glad she'd left him— they hadn't suited each other, hadn't enjoyed the same things. Susan had been right—they were best apart.

As he entered the house, Jodie and Peter came hurtling towards him. He caught Jodie up, swinging her round until she squealed, then pretended to growl at Peter like a bear. They had a mock fight until Susan came to claim her children.

'Up those stairs, you monsters!' Susan smiled fondly as she looked at her brother, and he knew she had taken note of the faint signs of strain in his face. She touched his hand in concern. 'You look tired, love. Send the brats to bed and have a drink.'

The children, having delved in Philip's pockets for the sweets he never failed to bring, ran away, clutching their treasures. They had been allowed to stay up on the understanding that they went to bed immediately after greeting him.

Philip went into the comfortable, slightly shabby sitting room. It had the lived-in look that all homes with children gradually acquired—books, toys and games overflowed from the tables and chairs, though the floor had been cleared in an effort to make it look tidy.

Mike was sitting in front of the TV, watching the news. He switched it off as Philip sat down, pulling a wry face.

'One of these days they'll think of something good to tell us,' he said. 'I sometimes think that if I see one more trouble spot, one more crying child, I'll go out and do something dreadful…'

'I know what you mean,' Philip agreed with a sigh. 'It's the children that get to me, too. Talking of which, you are coming on Friday night? To the darts match? We need you on the village side, Mike. You won't let us down?'

'Of course he won't,' Susan said, pressing a glass of his favourite red wine into her brother's hand. 'Would any of us dare after you've worked so hard to get sponsors for this event? Besides, I'm coming to cheer you all on. I've arranged a baby-sitter for the evening, and I'm looking forward to an evening out.'

'Good. I was hoping you might,' Philip said, giving

her an affectionate pat as she passed on her way back
to the kitchen. 'I've got Lady Rowen's party coming up
again, Susan—any ideas? You know what she's like for
having her table just so. Every man has to have a lady
with him. Is your friend June free by any chance? She
doesn't chatter too much…'

'Oh, didn't I tell you?' Susan paused on the threshold,
an odd look in her blue eyes. She was a pretty woman
with soft, curling hair and a good figure. 'June has found
a new man. It's a red-hot affair, by all accounts, so I
don't imagine she'll be free for New Year. I'd come with
you myself, but Mike's boss has invited us over to his
house—and that's tantamount to a royal command.' She
pulled a wry face.

'Think of someone, will you?' Philip said, giving her
a persuasive smile. He and his sister weren't at all alike
to look at. Philip's hair was much darker, almost black,
his eyes a serious grey. At thirty-three, he was still exceptionally good-looking—at least in his sister's admit-
tedly biased opinion—with just a sprinkling of grey at
the temples. He was lean and had an athletic look,
achieved with a minimum of effort on his part and envied by his brother-in-law, who had to watch a tendency
to gain weight. 'I don't know anyone who might be
free…except Miss Sexpot, and somehow I don't think
Lady Rowen would be pleased if I took Anne to a party
at her house.'

'She isn't still after you, is she?' Susan asked, pulling
a wry face. 'I know I'm always telling you to find someone—but not Anne Browne, Phil. She would eat you for
starters and then look for the main course. She's not your
type at all.'

'She is a bit of a man-eater,' Philip said, and laughed,

amused by his sister's frankness. 'It's a pity, really, because she's a nice girl in every other way.'

'I'm not sure I know anyone you could take to the party,' Susan said, looking thoughtful. 'Mary's going to America for three weeks over Christmas and New Year, and Beryl was a disaster the last time she was here. You asked me not to invite her again. Besides, I think she may have found a partner, too.'

'Oh, well, maybe I'll think of someone,' Philip said. 'I suppose I could always hire an escort from one of those agencies.'

'Phil!' His sister looked horrified. 'You wouldn't... No, of course not. You're pulling my leg again. Wretch!'

Susan disappeared into the kitchen to rescue a saucepan that had begun to boil over, and the two men settled down to a chat about local affairs. Much of it was to do with the new children's unit at the Chestnuts. They'd been raising funds for the past year, and were now approaching the sum of money needed to complete the work. Lady Rowen had not yet sent in her contribution, but she'd hinted that she would do so at her party, an annual event of some importance in the village.

'I've thought of someone,' Susan said as she came to call the men to the table. 'Do you remember Christine Barber? I think she may be staying with her parents over Christmas...'

Philip pulled a face. 'She's the one that laughs like a donkey, isn't she? No, please, don't do that to me, Susan. I think I really would rather use an escort agency.'

'You should find yourself a nice girl to go out with sometimes, and then you wouldn't be in this fix,' his sister said, frowning at him. 'Surely there must be someone available at the hospital. Isn't there anyone you like? No one at all?'

'Well…' Philip thought about Megan, about those wonderful legs and the wicked smile she had given Jennifer. 'There is someone who would be suitable…but I don't suppose she'd want to go…'

'You won't know unless you ask her.' Susan sighed with exasperation. He knew that sometimes she despaired of him. 'You haven't mentioned a lady friend before. Is she nice?'

Philip saw the look in her eyes and shook his head. 'Now, don't get ideas, Susan. We spoke for a few seconds this afternoon, that's all. Sister Hastings is new to the Chestnuts—though we did meet when I was at Guy's years ago.'

'An old flame…' Susan's eyes gleamed with interest. 'Do tell. When can I meet her?'

'It wasn't a love affair. We were much too young,' her brother said as he saw the gleam. Susan was putting two and two together and making five as usual. 'We went around in a crowd most of the time, then she asked me to a wedding—a family thing, I think. I couldn't go because I was playing squash—'

'You turned the poor girl down for a squash tournament?' Susan stared at him in dismay and disbelief. 'A family wedding and you refused to go! That sounds a bit selfish, not like the man I know and love. It wasn't very fair of you, Phil. I should think she had told everyone about you and was hoping to show you off to her family. Did she kick up a row over it? I know I would have.'

'She broke it off between us,' he said, looking rueful. 'I was annoyed at the time and didn't argue when she said we were finished. A few days later I tried to ring her to apologise, but I was told she had gone away. To be honest, I didn't follow it up. I had exams and then I met Helen…maybe the split with Megan had something to do with me falling for Helen so hard. I didn't meet anyone else I liked for months after Megan dumped me.'

'Hurt pride…' Susan smiled and shook her head at him. 'You always were stubborn and independent, Phil. Being dumped would have put you off women for ages. Anyway, you can forget asking Sister Hastings to be your partner for the party. I imagine your name is very definitely mud in that quarter.'

'Yes…' He had a sudden feeling of regret. Looking back, he realised the wedding must have been important to Megan. He ought to have been more understanding of her feelings. 'It was very bad of me. I shall have to apologise when I see her next…'

Philip sipped the small whisky he allowed himself at he end of a busy day, then set the glass on the bedside table while he did the press-ups he felt necessary to keep himself fit. Although blessed with the kind of metabolism that burned off excess calories, giving him a lean, hard body, the one game of squash he managed to fit in every week with his friend Matthew Keane wasn't enough to keep him as inwardly fit as he would have liked.

He no longer had the time to play rugby—it belonged to those heady, glorious days of being a medical student. Philip smiled as he remembered—he'd been full of ideals and enthusiasm then. He was still blessed with a great deal of energy, but it was devoted to his work these days. He moved in a very different world—committee meetings, prestige charity functions and practice business used up most of the hours not devoted to the care of his patients.

Susan grumbled that getting him to come to dinner was like booking an appointment with the managing director of a multinational company.

'You should take time to breathe like the rest of us mortals,' she'd told him recently. 'You're so wrapped up in your world, Phil. Time is ticking away. You should make more space for fun.'

Philip knew his sister was right. Sometimes he scarcely had time to breathe these days. Still, it stopped him thinking too much. There had been a time just after his divorce when he'd tended to brood on the meaning of life.

He'd indulged in a couple of casual sexual relationships, an instinctive reaction to finding himself free after Helen had walked out, but neither of them had been particularly satisfactory. Without love, sex wasn't all it was cracked up to be, at least not for him. Since then he'd contented himself with platonic friendships and his family.

Philip reviewed his day as he finished his drink, as was his custom, but work seemed far away. For some reason the sight of a pair of extremely good legs getting out of a car flashed into his mind.

She was a very, very attractive woman these days! She always had been, of course. There had been times when he'd felt very attracted to Megan. He smiled as he remembered one particular day by a river bank. He and Megan had taken a picnic to the river. They had swum together, then lain on a blanket in the sun, kissing and eating strawberries dipped in fizzy wine.

'I'll buy you champagne one day…'

Philip felt a jolt like a live wire touch his skin. Megan had kissed him and…they had come very close to making love. It had been he who'd drawn back, because he hadn't been ready to commit to a relationship at that time. His exams had been looming!

But the memory made him feel an acute longing. It was a while since he'd held a woman…made love to someone he really cared for. His thoughts dwelt on what it would be like to hold Megan now, to touch her…to feel her soft skin close to his own and…

'You've been living like a monk for too long,' he murmured to himself, amused at his own thoughts, which were wildly out of order. 'It's time you pulled yourself together.'

Philip's sense of humour came to the rescue, and he recovered his usual composure as he prepared for bed. It wasn't likely that a woman who looked as gorgeous as Megan Hastings would be without a partner, neither would she be well disposed towards a man who'd refused to go to a wedding with her because he'd been playing squash!

Had he really been that young and thoughtless? It was odd, but he'd never seen himself as the arrogant type— he simply liked to keep his thoughts to himself. He wasn't one of those men who spilled out their thoughts to anyone after a few drinks in the pub. In fact, he never went into a pub these days, unless it was to buy a bottle of whisky—or for a quick lunchtime drink with his brother-in-law on a warm summer Sunday.

Had his careless attitude hurt Megan that summer? When they'd met at the Chestnuts, she'd seemed to want to keep her distance, and he'd seen a slight hostility in her eyes. He was sorry if he'd hurt her all those years ago. He really would have to eat humble pie when he saw her again, Philip realised. If only because he was bound to meet her at the hospital now and then…

CHAPTER TWO

'GOD I hate you!' Matthew Keane cried as he lunged at the ball speeding past him and missed. 'That's another game you've won, damn you!'

Philip smiled as he looked at his opponent. Matthew had been his closest friend since they'd both been at boarding school together and the friendship had endured over the years. Despite the way their lives had diverged, Matthew going into accountancy and Philip to medical school, they'd always managed to keep in touch. And recently Matthew had moved to Granchester, which meant they were able to meet at least once a week, sometimes more.

'Your trouble is you're not fit enough,' Philip said, looking at his friend's flushed cheeks. 'Playing squash once a week isn't enough, Matt. You need to do some training—weights or running...'

'Have a heart,' Matthew said, pulling a wry face as he mopped the sweat from his brow. 'We're not all blessed with as much energy as you.'

'It's sitting in that office all day,' Philip said, frowning as he looked at him. 'No, I mean it, Matt. You ought to think about losing a stone—and cut down on your drinking.'

'Yeah, yeah,' Matthew said good-naturedly. 'So we'll all live for ever and they'll have to start a colony on the moon to get rid of us. Time for a drink this evening?'

'Yes, of course,' Philip said. 'I'll meet you in the bar after we've showered. It's my round this time.'

'I hadn't forgotten,' Matthew said, grinning at him. 'Seriously, Phil, I do try, but since the divorce...well, you know how it is.'

Philip nodded. He picked up his bag and headed for the showers. He wanted a swim in the pool, before joining Matthew in the bar, but he knew it was useless to invite his friend.

When Philip had changed and was feeling refreshed from his swim, he went through to the wine bar of the exclusive sports complex. Matthew was already there, drinking a gin and tonic. Philip started to cross the room, then a woman's laughter made him turn his head. Two women were seated at one of the tables—Megan Hastings and another woman he didn't recognise.

He hesitated, wondering whether to go over to her, then a man approached the table, carrying a tray of drinks. Megan looked up and smiled. She said something that made the man laugh, then she turned her head and looked across the room directly at Philip. She half smiled, but the man was sitting down and he said something that claimed her attention.

Philip frowned and walked over to join his friend. He had no idea that Megan had glanced his way again in time to notice the frown, neither that she had taken it for disapproval.

'I've started,' Matthew said as he reached him. 'Wine for you, Phil?'

'Just water,' Philip said. 'I like to drink plenty of water after a good workout. Besides, I'm driving.'

'So am I.' Matthew laughed. 'I shan't have more than my limit, so don't look like that, Phil. I shan't overdo it. My driving licence is too important. One more and then I'm off...unless you feel like having a meal?'

'Why not?' Philip said, knowing that with his divorce

so recently granted Matthew was feeling a bit disorientated. 'Yes, I'd like that, Matt.'

'She's a looker, isn't she?' Matthew said as Philip perched on the stool next to him. 'That gorgeous woman in the all-white kit over there. I think she must be a new member. I haven't seen her here before.'

'No, you wouldn't have,' Philip said, frowning again. Megan seemed to be enjoying herself with her friends, though why that should bother Philip he didn't know. She was perfectly entitled to her own life. 'She's a nurse—Sister Hastings. She's just started up at the Chestnuts.'

'You know her?' Philip nodded, and Matthew grinned. 'That puts her off limits, then. I wouldn't want to tread on your toes, Phil.'

'I know her—that's all, Matt.'

'But you're interested,' his friend said. 'I know you better than most, Phil. Other people may think you're a bit on the arrogant side, but I know what makes you tick. You're as human as the rest of us, even though you might think you're one of the immortals.'

Philip chuckled. 'There's nothing like a good friend for putting you in your place,' he said. 'While I've got you, Matt, I shall never fall in love with my own legend.'

Matthew grinned and started to tell him a rather salacious joke he'd heard recently. Neither of them noticed that Megan was looking their way, or that there was a distinctly unfriendly expression in her eyes...

Sister Hastings was in her office when Philip passed on his way to visit the men's post-operative ward a couple of days later. He saw her checking some lists on her desk, walked by, then doubled back and poked his head in the door, determined to get the apology over.

He noticed that she was wearing sensible shoes, and her uniform disguised her lovely shape, which was probably just as well considering the effect she would otherwise have had, not only on the male staff but probably the patients as well. However, nothing could have hidden the fact that she was a very attractive woman.

'My sister says I deserve to be hung, drawn and quartered,' he said, giving her a smile most people thought charming. 'Is it any use apologising?'

Sister Hastings looked up, frowned and shook her head. 'I'm sorry,' she said, clearly at a loss. 'Why are you apologising? I don't understand. What have you done that's so unforgivable?'

Philip advanced into the room. He hovered tentatively, not sure how to begin.

'It's bad enough that I didn't remember all the details the other day,' he said. 'But what I did when we knew each other years ago was unpardonably rude. I'm sorry. I ought to have gone to that wedding with you...'

'Yes, you should have. My family was expecting it.' Megan looked at him, and there was something close to a flash of pain in her eyes. 'I was very upset at the time. It was a very special day for me...'

'Then Susan was right,' Philip said. 'If it helps, I did regret it, Megan—and it did hurt, being dumped.'

'It might have hurt your pride,' she said, and there was a touch of pride in her own manner. 'You weren't in love with me. I was very innocent in those days. I made it all too easy for you, didn't I?' This time her eyes held a certain resentment. 'If a woman gives her heart too easily, men have a habit of trampling all over it...'

'I didn't think it was that bad.'

Megan smiled suddenly, and it was as if a ray of sunlight had suddenly pierced the winter gloom. 'No, of course not. I wasn't thinking of you just at that moment. You...us... It was just one of those things that happen when you're young and thoughtless. You rang my flat-mate and apologised, didn't you? Don't worry, I haven't been brooding about it all this time. Besides, we're two different people now. Older and wiser.' Again there was that flash of something in her eyes.

Philip thought that she might have been hurt by some-one.

'Ten...no, nearly eleven years older,' he said. 'We've grown up, haven't we, Megan? I hope I may call you that? I'm Philip, or Phil, if you prefer.'

'Off duty, of course,' Megan said, her professional manner taking over. Perhaps he had imagined the look of pain, but he didn't think so. 'But I think "Doctor" is best on the wards. Not that we shall be working to-gether often. I'm on the medical wards at the moment.'

'I come to visit my patients,' Philip said. 'Any work I do here is entirely voluntary, of course. Most of my patients are post-operative, but occasionally I have someone on the medical side. I believe you have Mrs Bettaway in G3? She had a stroke two nights ago. Is she making satisfactory progress?'

'For her age,' Megan said, glancing down at her notes. 'I was just thinking about her before you arrived. She seems to have lost the use of her left leg and arm, though her mind is clear. A very intelligent lady. She was asking me earlier when she could go home, but I understand she lives alone?'

'Yes, she does.' Philip frowned. He knew Mrs Bettaway very well, and respected her. She'd been a headmistress until about ten years earlier, and was still very active at the school. 'Being a bit difficult, is she? I was afraid of that. She is a very independent lady. She won't settle to being in hospital for long.'

'I doubt if she'll live alone again. Not unless the physio can help her regain full mobility. And the paralysis is severe. Dr Mowbray told me he feels it may be permanent. He thinks she's lucky to have come round at all—and he believes she may suffer another seizure quite soon.'

'I see. As bad as that, is it?' Philip nodded, looking thoughtful. 'It's so difficult in these situations. I'll have a word, see if she could go to her daughter's for a while. If not, it means finding her a place at a nursing home eventually, I suppose.'

'She won't like that,' Megan said. 'Her daughter's house would be best, if it's possible. As I said, she is at risk of further strokes.'

'Well, I'll have a word,' Philip said. He smiled and glanced at his watch. 'I'm going to pop in and see Mrs Bettaway now. I'll find time to visit her daughter later, but I shall have to get a move on. It was nice, having a chat. And thank you for being so understanding about me letting you down that time.'

Megan smoothed a stray lock of hair behind her ear. Philip thought the simple action incredibly erotic.

'Forget it happened,' she said, and treated him to a smile that temporarily took his breath away. 'I hope we'll be friends, Phil.'

'I suppose...' He hesitated, then laughed. 'I wondered... Actually, I was going to ask you out for dinner this Saturday evening, but perhaps that's asking too much?'

'I would have enjoyed it,' Megan replied, 'but I'm having dinner with Robert Crawley. His sister and I were friends way back. He asked me yesterday, and I agreed…'

'Oh, well, maybe another time, when I'm not taking evening surgery,' Philip said, glancing at his watch again. 'You never know, we may bump into each other at the sports club…'

'Perhaps,' Megan replied. 'I was there with some friends the other evening. I haven't joined yet. I'm not sure if I shall…'

'Oh, but you should,' Philip said. 'It's a pretty good crowd there—and we could do with some new members.'

'Well, I'll think about it.'

'Yes, do that.' She glanced at her watch as if anxious to get on, and he realised she wanted to call a halt to their conversation. 'If I don't stop chattering, I'm never going to get round.'

He walked away, feeling slightly disappointed that she'd turned down his invitation. Megan Hastings was someone he could talk to on a professional level, and it might have been nice, taking her for a meal, but Crawley hadn't wasted any time. He'd made it obvious he'd been interested from day one. Besides, he himself wasn't interested in getting involved, not really. He liked Megan, and there was something very appealing about her… Those legs were worth watching any day!

It wasn't just the legs, though. He'd found himself thinking about her often since their first meeting, though he wasn't exactly sure why.

Yes, if he were honest, he did know why he'd been thinking about Sister Hastings. She was a very attractive woman. It was a long, long time since any woman had made this big an impression on him, had got under his skin—a long time since he'd had erotic dreams.

He smiled at his own thoughts. He was letting his imagination run away with him. Robert Crawley wouldn't be the only man in the district to notice the newcomer in their midst. She would be a fool to give up her chances in that direction for the sake of a humble GP. And Megan was certainly no one's fool. He wasn't sure how to classify her just yet.

Class...that was the word he'd been looking for, Philip realised. It wasn't just the fascinating walk and the long legs. Megan Hastings had a lot more going for her.

She was friendly enough, yet there was a feeling that she was holding back, being a little reserved—perhaps because of what had happened in the past.

She wasn't still brooding over him having refused to go to a wedding with her, of course, but perhaps she'd felt some initial resentment when they'd met again. It would have been natural enough.

He rather thought she was a nurse dedicated to her career. She had to be twenty-nine or so, and she wasn't wearing an engagement ring. Neither had she been married—at least, if she had, she'd reverted to her maiden name.

And if she hadn't married before this, there had to be a reason. He imagined she was more interested in her work than marriage. If she didn't have a man in tow, it was because Megan Hastings wanted it that way.

He was quite sure she would have no difficulty in finding interested partners in this part of the world. It wasn't often that a woman who looked the way she did came to a small community like theirs.

Philip shook his head at himself. The sooner he stopped trying to work out what made Sister Hastings

tick and got down to some work himself, the better—
and yet he rather liked thinking about her and those legs!

Philip walked into the hospital community room.
Normally full of chairs and small tables, it had been
specially cleared for the big event, with a table for re-
freshments—strictly non-alcoholic—at one end and the
dartboard at the other. The room was already crowded
and a little over warm, with supporters of both teams
overflowing into the corridor and the annexe.

There was an atmosphere of excitement. Despite the
match being a charitable event, there was keen rivalry
between the hospital staff and the villagers.

'I think it's a wonderful idea, having a competition to
see who can score one hundred and eighty with nine
darts.' Staff Nurse Browne waylaid him, giving him a
coy look. 'I'm going to enter—will you be my partner?'

'I'm sorry, I can't,' Philip replied. 'I've already entered with my sister. Why don't you ask Dr Stevens?
You'd stand a good chance of winning with him.'

He ignored the invitation in her eyes. That girl had
bedroom eyes if anyone had, and they seemed to be
permanently set on green as far as he was concerned.
He'd been steadfastly ignoring that come-on look for
months now, but his reserve seemed to make the young
nurse even more determined to lure him into bed. She
probably had no thought beyond that, and if rumour
were to be believed she'd had affairs with half the men
on the medical staff. Philip wasn't one of them, and
didn't intend to be. However, short of being very rude
to her, which wasn't his way, there seemed no way she
was prepared to accept defeat.

He excused himself with a nod. He caught sight of
his sister and brother-in-law, and went to join them.

'Mike's playing your Sister Hastings,' Susan said, bubbling over with her news. 'We've just been talking to her. She's really nice. You must bring her for lunch one Sunday.'

'She isn't *my* sister Hastings,' Philip said wryly. 'I doubt if she's anyone's. I should say she's very much her own woman—a lady who knows what she wants in life.'

'Robert Crawley's taking her to dinner tomorrow,' Susan went on. 'She seems to have half the men here this evening running after her. Dr Morton was practically drooling over her a few minutes ago!'

'He's married.' Philip frowned as he glanced across the room. Megan was at the centre of an animated group consisting entirely of men. She appeared to be enjoying herself, and the men certainly were. 'You said she's on the hospital darts team?'

'Drawn against Mike,' Susan said. 'Sister Marsh used to play, if you remember. They needed another player. Sister Hastings volunteered to take her place.'

'I wonder if she's any good. Mike would have beaten Sister Marsh.'

He looked across at Megan again, trying to weigh her up as possible opposition.

This time she saw him and smiled. Philip nodded an acknowledgement but didn't smile. He wasn't sure why he was feeling a bit put out with her. It wasn't her fault if Morton was drooling over her—the old fool made a beeline for any woman who looked good in a skirt! She didn't have to respond to his flirting, though.

He must be getting old! Either that or he was jealous. Ridiculous! Philip felt a jolt of surprise. Why should he be jealous about a woman he hardly knew? He was aware that Megan had a powerful effect on his libido every time she was near him, but that wasn't so unusual, was it? He was a perfectly healthy male, and it had been a long time since he'd indulged himself in a love affair. But this was neither the time nor the place to indulge in such speculation.

Philip turned his thoughts to other things, deliberately squashing the temptation to join the men fluttering around Megan.

There were three matches scheduled that evening. The first, between Dr Morton and a young builder called Jack Marlowe, was already under way. As the organiser, Philip watched with interest. He was certain Marlowe would lose. If his father hadn't given such a generous contribution to the hospital fund, he would never have been picked for the team.

'I understand you're not playing…'

Philip hadn't noticed Megan approach. He turned to look at her, admiring what he saw. She had changed out of uniform, and was wearing black, straight-legged trousers, black ankle boots and a soft white sweater with a roll neck. The sweater didn't help to hide the perfect form underneath, or the fact that she seemed to exude sensuality from her pores. He liked her perfume, which was light and fresh, very feminine. He took a grip on himself before he started to drool.

'It's not really my game.'

'No. I remember…you were never interested.' She arched her brows. 'So why are you here tonight?'

'I organised the event this year.'

'Ah, I see. So who's next?'

'The landlord of the local pub…' Philip eyed her speculatively. 'And you're on last. Are you any good?'

Megan laughed, mischief in her eyes. 'Are you asking me to give team secrets away?'

'Yes. Will you?'

'No. You'll just have to wait and see.'

Her smile was intriguing. Philip was amused. Megan was no pushover, that much was plain.

'Oh, damn,' he groaned as Marlowe's darts went all over the board. 'He's useless.'

'I would say that was a fair description,' Megan said. She was smiling, confident. Her eyes met his in an open challenge. 'Why did you pick him? Did you think you had no competition?'

'His father sponsored him for a thousand pounds,' Philip replied honestly. 'Where the children's unit is concerned, I'm entirely open to bribes.'

'Yes, I've heard you've been the driving force behind it,' Megan said, looking at him with interest now. 'Any particular reason? Apart from the obvious, of course.'

'We need to accommodate more children here,' Philip said. 'Especially serious cases, which we don't have the facility for at the moment. I know there's the hospice at Milton, but that's a long way for parents who don't have a car. Besides, there's never enough room, never enough money, to treat everyone in the way we would like. So, if we can make things easier for just a few of the children and their families...' He shrugged and pulled a wry face. 'You've got me going on my hobby-horse, I'm afraid.'

'You really care, don't you?' She stared at him, as if seeing him properly for the first time. 'I like that, Phil. I mean, we all care—of course, we do—but you're dedicated.'

'Sometimes too much,' he said wryly. 'My wife said I ate, slept and breathed work. She was probably right to leave me. In fact, I'm sure she was.' He gave her a self-deprecating look. 'I dare say I wasn't fair to Helen.

I seem to have captured the first prize for arrogance where women are concerned, don't I?'

'Perhaps…' Megan's expression was giving nothing away. 'I suppose it can't be easy, living with a dedicated doctor—especially if you haven't worked in the profession yourself.'

'Yes. I understood her position perfectly,' Philip agreed, and laughed. 'I think at the end it was a relief to us both—'

There was a sudden cheer from the people around them, and he realised his attention had wandered away from the darts.

The first match had ended in a win for the hospital team. Philip clapped, nodded to Megan, then went over to Marlowe and laid a consoling hand on his shoulder.

'Better luck next time,' he said. 'Morton is a good player.'

The next match was between John Saunders, who ran the local pub, and Dr Stevens. Saunders was the best player they had, and the hopes of the village team lay mostly with him.

He scored three one hundred and eighties during the match, and won every leg. The result of Saunders's own match had always been predictable, and he left the stage to tumultuous applause. It was surprising how much noise a few people could make!

'All down to you now, Mike,' Philip said to his brother-in-law. 'You'll have to be good this evening. I have a feeling Megan Hastings may be a dark horse.'

His words were prophetic. Megan took the first set easily in three straight legs. The second went to Mike, mainly because Megan missed her doubles and let him in, but she took the third with ease.

The room erupted with cheers from the hospital supporters. Philip cheered and clapped as loudly as any of them. After all, the children's unit had gained from the event, and that was all he was concerned about.

Mike was gloomy, seeming to think it had been all his fault. 'Sorry to let you down, Phil. Can't think what went wrong.'

'You played as well as always,' Philip assured him. 'It was just that Sister Hastings is a brilliant player.'

'The result of a misspent youth,' Megan's voice said behind him, making him glance round. She was smiling, flushed with victory. 'I came to apologise for upsetting the apple cart. I understand your team was expected to win this evening. And to ask if I can buy you all a drink.'

'I'll have an orange juice,' Susan said, and grinned at her. 'Don't apologise, Sister Hastings. I think you were fantastic. And we women must stick together, don't you agree? It serves them right for not putting their best player in to bat against you. Mike would probably have beaten Dr Stevens.'

'And Megan would quite probably have beaten Saunders,' Philip said. 'But I'll have that drink before the pairs competition starts. Mine's a tomato juice—I'll come with you to fetch it.'

He watched as Megan ordered and paid for the drinks, then gave him two to carry. Her beauty would always bring her popularity where the men were concerned, but she had a lot more than just her looks going for her. He'd liked what he'd seen that evening. She was a very confident woman, pleasant and friendly, but nobody's fool.

Sister Hastings was obviously going to be an asset to the community in more ways than one.

Philip was restless, unable to keep his mind on the new paperback thriller he'd borrowed from Mike. He laid the book down, walking over to the window to gaze out at the front garden, which was lit by the bright moonlight. The weather was milder and the bushes looked damp, dripping with moisture, singularly unappealing.

He wasn't really a gardening man, not a plantsman, though he mowed lawns and weeded the rose beds in the summer. Being out there was pleasant on a warm Sunday morning because there was always someone to stop for a chat.

Good grief! Was he feeling lonely? He frowned, considering the idea. Usually, he found his life fulfilling, seeming never to have enough hours in the day for all he wanted to do. But this last couple of days he'd been aware of a new restlessness, a feeling that he wanted more out of life.

Of course, there had been a time when he'd wanted children, a proper family to come home to at night, but he'd put all that behind him when Helen had left.

Philip laughed at himself. It was women who were supposed to get broody! He didn't need children of his own—he had Susan's to spoil. Mike and his sister were very generous in sharing their offspring. He knew he was expected to celebrate Christmas Day with them, and would be welcomed in their home for as much of the rest of the festive season as he cared to spend there.

That reminded him! He had to start planning his Christmas present list. The children always made their wants plain, so it was easy enough to find things for them, but he wanted to get something nice for his sister—and there were his partners, Henry and James, and their wives. He would be invited to their homes during the next few weeks. It was a routine that never failed, and he liked to give them something they would appreciate rather than just wine or chocolates.

Yes, it was time he popped into Cambridge to start his shopping. If he went soon he would avoid the seasonal crowds.

Maybe mid-week, he thought. He returned to his book, but the print seemed to blur into meaningless blobs. He wondered if Megan was enjoying her night out with Robert Crawley...

Oh, well, he may as well give the book up as a bad job and go to bed. In the morning he thought he'd go and visit Matthew, take him out for a decent meal, then maybe they'd go to the gym and work out. They could both do with the exercise.

Philip picked up a brochure for winter holidays he had sent for, and took it upstairs with him. Somehow he had to fit in a few days' skiing soon. Perhaps between Christmas and the New Year...

It was late in the afternoon when he left Matthew the next day. His friend had seemed in a more cheerful frame of mind, and had told him he'd met a new woman. He'd asked her to go to the theatre with him, and was looking forward to taking her out.

'Good, I'm glad you're beginning to feel better,' Philip had said. 'Now you can start on that diet I mentioned...'

He'd dodged the punch Matthew had aimed at him, and was still smiling to himself as he drove home. The break had done him as much good as it had Matthew, and he was thinking about a charity meeting he was due to attend the next day.

He stopped off at the pub in the village to pick up a bottle of whisky, then left, intending to have a quick bath and change, because he was on call that evening. As he emerged from the pub he saw a woman getting out of Robert Crawley's car, and recognised her at once.

He knew Megan had dined with Crawley the previous evening, and it crossed his mind that she might have spent the night and that morning with him. The idea was so unappealing that, instead of waiting to greet her, he merely waved, got into his car and drove off.

Philip couldn't imagine why he was so interested in Megan's comings and goings. It wasn't as if he'd ever really known her, not even when they'd both been training in London.

Philip laughed at himself, dismissing his thoughts as ridiculous. Why on earth was he allowing himself to become so interested in a woman he hadn't thought about for years? It wasn't like him…it wasn't like him at all.

It was time he went home and started to think about work for a change!

'We'll start you on the tablets today, Mrs Raven,' Philip said, and gave her the leaflets that would tell her more about her diabetes. 'You don't need insulin. It's what they call diabetes mellitus, maturity onset or Type II. It can usually be controlled by a combination of diet and the tablets, and we'll keep a check on your blood here so you won't have to go to the hospital every time. You can do the urine tests yourself—it's only a matter of using a little plastic stick.'

'But I've never been good at dieting. All that weighing and measuring,' she said with a sigh. 'And I love chocolate, Doctor. I just don't know if I can give it up entirely.'

'I've made an appointment with the dietician for you

for tomorrow,' Philip said. 'She'll help you to sort out a diet that you can follow. It's really just a matter of being sensible, Mrs Raven. You don't need to weigh everything, believe me. If you do eat a small piece of chocolate now and then it won't kill you, but keep it for high days and holidays. We always tell our patients to avoid all sugary foods, but we know they slip now and then—it isn't the end of the world. It's just trying to achieve a balance.' He smiled at her encouragingly as she got up to leave.

'I shall see you again next week. Be sure to make an appointment before you leave the surgery—and if you feel ill or if you're worried, give me a ring. At home if need be.'

'You're so kind,' she said, a smile lighting up her faded blue eyes. 'I honestly don't know what we would do without you, Dr Grant. You've always got time to listen.'

'That's what I'm here for,' he said. 'Now, look on the bright side. If you lose weight you can go out and buy some new clothes, make yourself look good for the glamorous granny competition next spring. There's another three weeks to Christmas, and the contest is in March—plenty of time to get yourself in shape. I'll bet you were a stunner when you were sixteen.'

'I was, that,' she said. 'I had all the men after me.'

'Keep to your diet, and you will again.'

Mrs Raven started giggling like a teenager and went out of the surgery with a spring in her step.

Philip finished entering her notes into his computer, then buzzed for his next patient. He saw three more that evening—a case of bronchitis, a cut which had become infected and what he suspected was grumbling appendicitis. He referred the young woman to the hospital, putting her on the semi-urgent list. She was in some pain, and it would be best to operate before the condition became acute.

With the waiting room empty at last, Philip went through his notes, before saving his work and shutting down the computer. It was only then that he glanced at his watch and saw the time. Nearly eight-thirty. He'd run over by almost an hour again!

Picking up his briefcase, he went out to the reception area and caught the long-suffering Mrs Brodie yawning over a magazine.

'I'm so sorry,' he apologised. 'I've kept you late again, haven't I?'

'You always do,' she said, giving him a smile that took the sting from her words. 'Never mind, Doctor. I saw some happy faces leaving the surgery. I'm sure it was all worthwhile.'

'You get off,' Philip said. 'I've got a couple of things to do and then I'll lock up. I'll find some way of making it up to you one day.'

'I'm quite happy, Doctor,' she said, apparently willing to linger for a chat. 'I heard you won your match the other night. Pity the village lost, but it seems Sister Hastings played a mean game of darts.'

'She certainly did,' Philip replied, smiling as he re-membered. 'But we raised three thousand pounds for the fund. We may have lost the match, but at least we've almost reached our target for the new unit—and that's what matters.'

After she'd gone, Philip sorted out some papers he wanted, then locked the door and went out to his car. It was ten minutes to nine, and the surrounding countryside was pitch black once he left the village streetlights be-hind.

Fortunately, he saw the warning triangle before he came up to the car. Someone had broken down, and had had the sense to put up the reflective triangle that had caught his lights. He slowed down as he went by, then stopped when he saw a woman staring helplessly at a flat tyre.

'Can I help?' he asked, getting out of his car and going over to her. 'Having trouble, Megan?'

'I bought this car last Saturday,' Megan said, pulling a wry face. 'I noticed one of the tyres looked a bit worn at the time, but they promised to replace it. When I collected it they said they hadn't had time but the new tyre was in the boot...'

'You should have refused to take delivery,' Philip said, frowning as he shone a torch on the tyre. 'This looks defective, and could have been dangerous.'

'Yes, I know.' She bit her lip, obviously upset at what had happened. 'Unfortunately, I'm not much good at changing tyres. I always keep mine in good order and have them checked at the garage regularly. I was in a hurry when I collected the car or I would have insisted they change it then.'

'I should demand another tyre,' Philip said, looking grim. 'Your spare should be roadworthy as well, so that's no excuse for them sending you out with a new tyre in the boot. But I'll change this for you. Then you must promise to take the car back first thing and make them give you a new spare.'

'Yes, Doctor.' Megan sounded as if she was annoyed. 'I assure you, I'm not usually this foolish...'

'Oh, dear, was I lecturing you?' Philip laughed ruefully. 'It's a bad habit of mine. Susan tells me I do it all the time. She says I sometimes talk to her as if she's a twelve-year-old. It's completely unintentional, believe me.'

'I wasn't meaning to reprimand you,' Megan said, watching as he took the jack from the boot of his own car and got down to work. 'To be honest, I'm annoyed with myself. It's very kind of you to help me. I'm not sure what I would have done if you hadn't come along. I was thinking of abandoning the car and walking home.'

'Where do you live?' Philip asked. He nodded as she mentioned she was renting a cottage in the village, then frowned as he rolled the defective tyre away. 'This is in a disgusting state. I'll have a word with the garage for you, if you like. I think they should be ashamed of themselves. I'm not sure this tyre is even legal.'

'Don't worry,' Megan said in a tone that brooked no argument. 'They will replace the tyre and apologise tomorrow.'

Philip looked up at her and, seeing the militant glint in her eyes, he laughed. 'Good for you! Some people think they can take advantage of your sex. It will do them good to discover they're wrong. I like a woman who can take care of herself.'

'In most things,' Megan admitted, a little ruefully. 'I've always been hopeless with anything to do with cars, other than driving, of course. I suppose I should go to night school and learn how to change a tyre, shouldn't I?'

'I'll come round one Sunday and show you if you like,' Philip offered. He tightened the nuts on the new wheel, then replaced the jack. 'At least this tyre is decent, and I've checked the others on the car. You shouldn't have any trouble for a while now—but you will get a new spare, won't you?'

'Yes, of course.' She hesitated, then said, 'It looks as if I owe you another drink.'

'Why don't we meet next Sunday?' Philip suggested. 'If you're free, we could have a drink together somewhere, then…have lunch with Susan, if you could bear it. She did tell me to ask you, but somehow I didn't get around to it. I must warn you, she has two tearaways that go under the name of Jodie and Peter.'

'I wouldn't mind that, of course. It's just that…' Megan seemed to consider for a moment, then nodded. 'I liked Susan a lot,' she said. 'I'd enjoy the chance to meet her on her home ground. Thank you for asking me—and for helping me.'

'It was no trouble,' Philip said. 'I'm glad I happened to be here at the right time. It was only because I was running late again at the surgery.'

'You've only just finished?' Megan arched her brows, seeming surprised. 'Pretty late, isn't it? Don't you ever take time off for yourself?'

'Oh, now and then,' he said. 'I go to the sports complex sometimes, as you know, and I like to ski when I can get away. But work takes up most of my time, of course. There's evening surgery five nights a week, but I usually have Saturday and Sunday evenings free. Though I am sometimes on call over the weekend…'

'Oh, well,' she said with a look of resignation. 'It's the job, I suppose. I used to grumble about hospital hours once, but they're pretty good at the Chestnuts. We all get regular time off.'

'Where did you work before you came here?'

Philip was wiping his hands on a rag. He didn't see her expression, but sensed her hesitation and looked up.

'In Manchester,' she said. 'A large hospital, very different to the Chestnuts. Why do you ask?'

'No particular reason, just asking…'

'If you've heard gossip…' There was a hint of anger in her eyes, and her head went up defiantly.

'I never listen. And if I do, I ignore it.'

She gave him an odd, rather resentful stare. 'Of course, you would. As you said, you don't listen to gossip. You live on another plane to the rest of us, don't you? The dedicated doctor, fighting to save humanity…'

'Hey, what have I done to deserve that?' He looked at her in bewilderment. 'I'm sorry if I said something out of turn.'

'No…' Megan bit her lip. 'It wasn't really you, just…' She shook her head, deciding she'd said too much. 'Well, I must go. I'm expecting a phone call. Thank you again…'

Philip wondered what he'd said to make her angry again. Why had she asked if he'd been listening to gossip? Was there something she didn't want him to know?

Philip thought about Megan a lot that evening. He was glad he'd been able to help her out, and angry that the garage had treated her so shabbily. He wished she'd given him permission to speak to the salesman who had sent her out with that defective tyre. He wouldn't do it again in a hurry!

But, of course, Philip couldn't interfere. Megan had made it perfectly clear that she was capable of handling it herself. Perhaps she'd had to learn to do things for herself—she was clearly used to being in charge of her own affairs. He wondered about her past life. The Chestnuts was a good place to work, but it wasn't exactly the pinnacle of success for a professional woman.

And since she didn't seem to have anyone special in

her life, it would seem her work was all-important to her.

Why had she decided to leave Manchester to come here? He wondered, but nothing came to mind. Yet there had been something in her tone…in her eyes…which had suggested she hadn't been comfortable, talking about her past.

CHAPTER THREE

PHILIP was having coffee with Dr Stevens in the hospital canteen the next afternoon when he heard two nurses talking.

'She's been working abroad for a year,' one nurse said. 'They say there was some kind of trouble at the hospital in Manchester. Apparently, she was asked to leave…'

Philip turned his head to watch as they left the canteen together. One of them had been Staff Nurse Browne.

'Were they talking about Sister Hastings?' He arched his brows at his companion. 'She told me about being in Manchester, but not about working abroad…'

'Africa, I'm told,' James Stevens said with a frown. 'I believe she contracted a nasty virus out there and was advised to return to the UK—at least, that's what the grapevine says. I don't know why she went out there, I'm afraid. However, her record must be OK or they wouldn't have taken her on here. You know what our board is like. Whatever happened in Manchester, it couldn't have been all that terrible.'

Philip nodded. He also knew what the gossips were like in a small community like this. People heard half a tale and made up the rest. Having spoken to Megan several times now, he believed her to be a very honest and professional woman.

'She's very good at her work,' James Stevens went on. 'Over-fussy at times, or so Morton says. She insists on checking every dosage he prescribes twice with him, and questions anything she isn't one hundred per cent certain about. It got to him the first few times, I can tell you, but now he seems to admire her for it. Says she's one of the best nurses he has ever worked with, here or in London.'

'Well, she seems very straight to me,' Philip replied. 'I must say I like her.'

He was thoughtful as he drove back to the surgery a little later. It no longer seemed odd that Megan had momentarily frozen when he'd casually asked her where she'd worked before coming to Cambridgeshire. She'd obviously known there was gossip going the rounds. Something must have happened in Manchester, but Stevens had been right—it couldn't have been so very terrible or they wouldn't have taken her on at the Chestnuts.

Lady Rowen was on the board, and she would have rooted out anything in the least suspicious—a real terrier, that particular lady! Besides, Megan didn't strike him as the sort of woman who would lie to cover up her past.

His thoughts came full circle to Lady Rowen's New Year's Eve party. He was still no nearer to deciding who to ask as his partner, and Susan had been unable to come up with any names.

He could always ask Megan, of course. It was a natural progression from asking her to lunch at his sister's house. He wasn't sure why he hadn't done it before now. Except that she'd turned down his first dinner invitation.

That had been before the darts fixture, of course, and the incident of the tyre. Perhaps she would give a different answer if he asked her out again, though a dinner somewhere pleasant and intimate was very different to a family lunch, which would make her feel safe.

Was it because Megan had given him warning signals, telling him not to approach too closely, that he was interested?

Philip felt an odd tingle at the base of his neck. Watch out, it seemed to say. You could be getting in too deep here.

He frowned as he parked his car and went into the surgery. Just where was all this going? A drink at a pub and a family lunch was one thing, but if he went on inviting Megan out, it was bound to develop into something more than he'd intended.

His first invitation had been meant as an apology. Asking her to lunch had been in response to her tentative offer of a drink. It would have been rude not to respond, but he wasn't quite sure where he wanted to go from here.

'Ah, there you are, Philip,' one of his partners accosted him as he entered the reception area. 'I've been called out to a patient with a suspected heart problem. My list isn't very long—do you think you can cover for me until I get back?'

'Yes, of course, Henry,' Philip said. 'I'll see both lists alternately to try and even up the wait for everyone. You will come back before the end of surgery if you can?'

'Yes, of course—if I can. Knowing you, you'll still be hard at it when I get back. Sylvia was asking about you this morning. She wants to know when you're coming to dinner again.'

'Oh, soon,' Philip said. 'Nearer Christmas, perhaps?'

'We'll fix it up,' Dr Henry Robinson said. 'I don't like this weather much, do you? Too mild for the time of year, and wet. I prefer it crisper and colder, more seasonal. Less cases of flu then...'

Philip nodded, and went into his surgery. His own list

was as heavy as usual. If he had to see all Henry's patients, he would be here until well past eight again. And Mrs Brodie was on the desk. He would have to buy her a present...or take her to Lady Rowen's party. He considered the idea. She might like to go. He would mention it later and hear what she had to say.

Philip gave the cortisone injection and then wiped the patient's shoulder with sterile cotton wool soaked in an antiseptic lotion to combat the risk of infection.

'That should help reduce the pain,' he told the young woman. 'If you attend the physiotherapy clinic up at the hospital, they'll teach you exercises to help you regain the use of your frozen shoulder. The injection helps probably two out of three patients, but you have to help yourself as well—and you ought to think about changing your job. It's my opinion that this is an RSI problem, caused at least in part by sitting at your desk too long. It may be the position you adopt for work on your computer.'

'Yes, I know,' she replied. 'It's much worse if I spend too many hours at the computer. I've been thinking of looking for work elsewhere, but I'm getting married soon and I need the money. I earn more where I am than I could in a shop.'

'Well, think about it,' Philip said. 'And if you experience pain or swelling in your shoulder, come back to me at once. You shouldn't have any trouble, but there's always a slight risk of infection with any injection.'

She thanked him, pulled her blouse back over her shoulder, then picked up her coat and departed.

Philip checked that she'd been the last patient. It was a quarter past eight. Henry hadn't returned until half an hour ago, just in time to see the last of his patients.

'I'm sorry, Mrs Brodie,' Philip said to the receptionist as he went out. 'Late again.'

'Not to worry, Doctor. It wasn't your fault. My husband knows to expect me when he sees me.'

'I was wondering...' Philip hesitated, then shook his head. 'What are you doing for Christmas and the New Year, Mrs Brodie? Anything nice?'

'Yes, we are over the New Year,' she replied. 'We always have Christmas at home, but we're going away for the New Year—to the Bahamas. It's our twentieth wedding anniversary and Mr Brodie says we both deserve a treat for having made it so far.'

'That sounds wonderful,' Philip said. 'I wish I were coming with you.'

'That's what you should do, Doctor,' she replied, shaking her head at him. 'You work far too hard. I told Mr Brodie so, but he says you're not the sort to sit at home and twiddle your thumbs—you're not a shirker. Not like some I could mention.'

She clamped her mouth shut, as if realising she'd said just a little too much.

Philip smiled, and locked the surgery door behind them. His partner wasn't exactly a shirker, but tended to get away with as much as he could. Philip intended to make sure Henry made up for this evening. There was no way he intended to be on call this Sunday.

He was looking forward to taking Megan to his sister's house. In fact, in his own time he'd been thinking of nothing else since she'd agreed to go.

When he got into his car, he decided not to go home immediately. He felt like a little company that evening. He would visit the gym and work out for a while. If he was going to take that skiing trip after Christmas, he'd need to be in shape.

As he drove further through the village he saw Robert Crawley's BMW pulled up outside the cottage Megan Hastings was renting. She was seeing rather a lot of the farmer, wasn't she?

Philip was aware that he disliked the idea of them having a relationship, but was unable to analyse his reasons for feeling as he did. After all, Megan was a free agent, entitled to have as many friends as she chose.

She was just getting out of Crawley's car as he passed them, and he caught a glimpse of her legs in his headlights.

She did have very nice legs, he thought, smiling to himself as he thought of the weekend to come. He was looking forward to it. Of course, he wasn't thinking of a serious involvement himself. No thoughts of marriage. He'd made up his mind about that long ago.

Robert Crawley might be looking for a wife, though. He'd been a widower for five years now. He'd had a bit of a reputation as a flirt before his wife had died, and had played the field in the past few years, but he could have fallen hard this time. It was possible he was serious.

For a few moments Philip wondered why the idea of Megan Hastings marrying the farmer was so appalling…then he turned his car onto the main road and headed out towards the sports club. There was no point in dwelling on the thought. He couldn't be a dog in the manger, and he certainly wasn't looking for a wife himself.

Philip was in Boots just off the marketplace in Cambridge. He'd been hovering by the perfume counter for several minutes, trying to make up his mind which gift set to buy for Mrs Brodie. He liked the Elizabeth

Arden Red, but the sales assistant had been telling him that the Blue Grass range was probably a better buy.

'And who's the lucky lady?'

Philip turned as he heard the woman's teasing, husky voice, recognising it at once, and the smell of her own perfume, which was very distinctive.

'It's a present for my receptionist,' he said, looking rueful. 'She never complains when I keep her late at the surgery, and I want to give her something nice. We give her something from the practice at Christmas, of course, but this is just to show my personal appreciation.' He arched his brows. 'What do you think—the Blue Grass or the Red?'

'How old is she?' Megan asked, apparently interested in his problem. 'Either set is lovely, but the Blue Grass might appeal more to an older woman perhaps.'

'That's the one, then,' Philip said, feeling relieved at having the decision made for him. 'Thanks for the help. I don't usually dither, but I wanted to get it right.' He smiled at her. 'I thought it was time I started Christmas shopping. If I leave it all until the last minute, the shops here are murder.'

'I came in to get a few things I want to send abroad,' Megan said. 'I have a sister in South Africa. I usually send her pretty undies from M&S—she loves them and they're easy to post.' She smiled her amusement as she saw he already had several parcels on the floor at his feet. 'You look as if you've been busy this morning.'

'Yes. I've been lucky, actually. I managed to get most of what I wanted. The children's things are being delivered to my home, of course. I've got a new doll's pram for Jodie and a bike for Peter—besides the Beanies, space robots and all the rest. I like them to have several parcels to open—and I like to watch. That's the best bit of Christmas, isn't it? Apart from the carol service at King's, of course. I always watch that on the telly.'

Megan's brows rose. 'Lucky Peter and Jodie! It sounds as if you spoil them.'

'That's what Susan says,' Philip agreed with a laugh. 'I suppose I do. But Christmas is for kids, don't you think?'

'Yes.' Megan's smile was a little fixed. 'My sister has three, but I seldom see them. I can't buy toys or clothes because they grow up so fast. I have to send money.'

'That isn't as much fun, is it?'

His eyes were watchful. She was good at hiding her feelings, but sometimes didn't quite manage it in time.

'No,' she agreed, and there was a slight shadow in her eyes.

He wondered if he'd been right in thinking she was a career-woman—perhaps there was a secret tragedy in her past, some reason she'd never married. She seemed to regret not having children. Or perhaps he was making up his own explanations.

She sighed, adjusting her shoulder-bag. 'Oh, well, I'll let you get on with your shopping.'

'I've finished for today,' Philip said quickly before she could move away. 'Would you like to have coffee? I thought I might stop for one before I go home.'

'I'd love to come with you,' she replied, 'but I'm meeting someone for lunch. I'm sorry. It would have been nice.'

'Another time, then,' he said, wondering if her friend was a man. She looked very smart but she always did, even on duty. 'You're still on for Sunday, I hope?'

'Yes, of course. I'm looking forward to it.'

'So am I,' he said. 'I'll give you a lesson in changing tyres later on if the weather isn't too bad, shall I?'

'Yes, thank you,' she said. 'Sorry I can't stay…'

Philip watched her walk away. He was finding her more and more intriguing. Had she cut short their chat because she'd promised to have lunch with someone, or had he said something to disturb her again?

Philip visited Mr Jarvis at the hospital for perhaps the last time that afternoon. The elderly man feeling very much better—confident of managing his routine and eager to go home. After talking to him for a few minutes, Philip agreed with the hospital's diagnosis.

'I don't see why you shouldn't be able to go home tomorrow,' he said. 'I'll stop by and see how you're getting on after a few days. There's no need for you to come to the surgery just yet unless you wish to. Home visits would be more useful for the time being.'

After leaving the men's ward, Philip went to see Mrs Bettaway. She was looking brighter than on his earlier visits, and told him that her daughter was coming to take her home at the end of the next week. She would need a wheelchair and a nurse would come in to help dress her in the mornings, but everyone agreed she was getting on much better than had been expected.

'Eileen said you'd been to see her,' the elderly lady said. 'Her husband has brought a single bed downstairs for me. It's just a temporary arrangement, of course. I shall go home as soon as I can get going.'

'We'll see how you go on,' Philip said gently, knowing that she might never be fit enough to live alone again. 'You know what the tortoise said—slow but sure.'

'I was always a hare,' she replied, smiling, 'but Sister Hastings has been talking to me, telling me that I mustn't expect too much. She's a sensible woman. I like her—

and she's right. I suppose there comes a time when we all have to slow down.'

Philip agreed. He continued to sit, talking to her for several minutes before taking his leave. She was a delightful lady, and if will alone could do it she'd return to her own home one day. He was glad Megan had taken such an interest in Mrs Bettaway. Her talk had obviously done some good, helping the old lady to adjust. He had done his best to lift her spirits, but sometimes a woman understood another woman's mind better than a mere man could.

He'd hoped he might see her, but when he called at her office she wasn't there. One of the nurses told him that she'd gone home an hour or so earlier.

As he drove home himself, he noticed that it was turning cooler again. The road was actually quite frosty in places where the trees overhung the roads.

Philip was on call that evening. It should have been Henry's turn, but Philip had agreed to take it on, providing he was free on Sunday. It didn't bother him that he was likely to be called out during the evening—he had nothing in particular to do. But tomorrow was different.

Megan had changed shifts with a friend that afternoon so that she could leave early. He wondered if she was going out to dinner with Robert Crawley again that evening, and thought it likely. There wasn't a great deal of entertainment to be had in the area, unless you went into Cambridge, of course. The university town had a variety of cinemas, the Arts Theatre, which sometimes put on very worthwhile productions, and a couple of nightclubs.

Was Megan the kind of woman who liked to go dancing? The hospital always put on a decent dinner and dance the week before Christmas. He seldom bothered to attend, but always bought a couple of tickets because it was for a good cause.

He might ask Megan if she would like to go with him this year.

He was thinking about her, wondering about that look of sadness in her eyes when she'd spoken of not seeing her sister's children, as he parked his car and went into the cottage, switching on all the lights as he went because it made the place seem warmer.

The cottage was at least a hundred years old, but when Philip had bought it he'd had a lot of improvements made—central heating, insulation and newly plastered ceilings and walls. He'd chosen a plain beige carpet throughout, ringing the changes with rich colours in the drapes, leather chesterfield and wing chairs. The rest of the furniture was antique oak, complemented by the shining brass that stood in the open fireplace and on the side table in the hall. Thankfully, his cleaning lady came twice a week to keep it all in order!

Philip cooked himself a simple meal of steak with a jacket potato—done in the microwave—and a salad, and drank a half a glass of shandy, forgoing wine or spirits because he might be called out later.

He selected a CD and put it on the player. His sound system was state of the art and Susan said it looked like something an American space station might build into their rockets. It certainly had a wonderful sound, and Philip settled to listen to the soft music as he flicked through the winter holiday brochure again. A few days in Austria was just what he needed…or maybe he would go for a French resort this trip…

At seven that evening he was called out to a child with asthma, who had mislaid his inhaler while out playing and was having an attack. Philip supplied a replacement from the surgery, and spent some time calming the mother who was a rather nervous type.

The telephone was silent for the next two hours. When he answered it, he was surprised that the voice belonged to Megan Hastings and not the surgery's answering service.

'I'm sorry to call you out,' Megan said, 'but my neighbour has fallen and hurt himself badly. He's breathing but unconscious, and I think there may be damage to the spine. I've tried calling the ambulance service, but they say there'll be a possible delay of up to half an hour...'

'Right, give me the address and I'll be there in a few minutes.'

Philip checked in with his answering service to let them know where he was going, put through a call to the ambulance centre himself, then went out to his car. It was a bitterly cold night, and he used his de-icer spray on the windscreen, before turning the heater on full blast.

When he reached the patient's home Megan was with the elderly man and his wife, who was in tears. The man had just that minute come round, and Megan was trying to calm him, telling him to lie still until the doctor had examined him.

'I think he has a broken clavicle,' Megan said, 'but I can find no evidence of damage to the spine itself. I've made sure he hasn't been moved, just in case.'

'Best to be sure,' Philip said, giving her an approving look. 'You did the right thing calling me out, Megan. I've put through a call to Addenbrookes, and they'll be ready for him.'

'W-what's going on?' asked the man. 'Ellie...where are you?'

'Had a nasty fall, did you?' Philip asked, kneeling

down beside the patient, who seemed a little dazed. 'Can you tell me your name?'

'Bill Jones,' the patient said, sounding belligerent. 'I haven't gone daft, Doctor. It was only a slip on those wretched stairs.'

'Be quiet, Bill,' his tearful wife said. 'Dr Grant is only doing his job. You were unconscious for several minutes. I thought you'd stopped breathing, and I went next door for Sister Hastings. She gave you the kiss of life…'

Philip looked at Megan, who nodded. 'Well, done,' he said. 'It was extremely fortunate for Mr Jones that you happened to be in this evening.'

'Yes, it was fortunate,' she said. 'I believe that's the ambulance now. You must have more influence with them than I have, Dr Grant.'

She went to let the paramedics in, leaving Philip to tell them what he had discovered from his initial examination while she talked to the distraught Mrs Jones.

A head-restraint collar was fitted, the patient was lifted onto a stretcher and then carried out to the ambulance. Philip went with them to see Mr Jones safely installed, then he turned to Mrs Jones. She suffered from arthritis, and he knew she would find it very uncomfortable, riding in the ambulance.

'Would you like to go with your husband? Or would you prefer me to take you in my car?'

'I can do that,' Megan said. 'It's no trouble, and you may be needed in the village again before you could get back here.'

'I'll go with Sister Hastings,' Mrs Jones said. 'It was ever so kind of you to offer, Doctor, but I mustn't take you away in case someone else needs you. Besides,

Sister was so good earlier. I don't know what I would have done without her.'

'Are you sure you don't mind?' Philip asked, looking at Megan. 'Drive carefully. The roads are very slippery tonight.'

'Yes, Doctor.' Megan's eyes sparkled with amusement. 'I promise you, I'll be very careful. You really don't need to worry about me, you know.'

Philip caught the note of mockery in her voice, appreciating her sense of humour. 'Doing it again,' he murmured softly, but she heard him and nodded, smiling good-humouredly. He turned his attention to the elderly lady. 'I'll be in touch soon, Mrs Jones. Try not to worry too much. Mr Jones is going to the best place, believe me.'

He stood, watching, as the elderly lady switched off the lights and locked the door after her. Megan was beside her all the time, gently reminding her of what needed to be done and reassuring her.

She had an excellent manner, which made patients feel comfortable with her. And he had now seen for himself that she was more than merely competent at her job. Whatever had happened in Manchester, it couldn't have been because she'd been careless.

Philip frowned as he got into his car to drive home. If she hadn't been asked to leave because of her work, had it been something to do with a man? Liaisons between nurses and doctors were sometimes frowned on by the managers of hospital boards, particularly if one of the participants happened to be married to someone else.

Was that the secret Megan guarded so well? Was she involved with a married man?

It was possible, of course, but the young girl he remembered would never have broken up another woman's marriage. He distinctly recalled her having told him once that it had happened to someone she'd known and she had been very upset about it.

Philip knew she might have changed—people did—but somehow he didn't want to believe it…

He half expected a phone call from Megan later that evening. He thought she might have phoned him when she got home, just to let him know what the results had been on the tests Mr Jones would have undergone, but his phone remained silent.

He received no more call-outs that night, which was lucky as it snowed during the early hours. However, when the sun came up the next morning it disappeared as if it had never been.

He was glad not to have had to go out again during the snowstorm. He stayed by the fire until well past midnight, listening to dreamy music, then went to bed. Years of being on call had left their mark, and he had a knack of waking as soon as the telephone rang. It was by his bed, and had an extra-loud bell.

He spent the early morning reading the papers and eating the toast which was all he allowed himself when he was eating out later. Susan's Sunday lunches were legendary!

At eleven he took a shower, and dressed in the clothes he intended to wear that day. It was an informal occasion so he chose jeans, a black silk and wool sweater Susan had given him on his birthday and a rather worn but much-loved suede jacket. His sister had been on to him to buy a new one for ages, but he'd never found another that was as comfortable to wear.

Glancing in the mirror to check that he looked decent, he saw a couple of grey hairs. He frowned, annoyed with himself for even noticing. Were they a sign of approaching middle age? Or could he dismiss them as merely a mark of distinction? They wouldn't have bothered a woman like Megan, of course. Robert Crawley must be nearing forty, and was already quite grey at the temples.

'Hey, what's wrong with you?' he asked his reflection. 'I thought it was the female of the species who was supposed to be vain?'

He laughed at himself, realising that until these last few days he couldn't have cared less what anyone thought about his appearance or his age. It just showed that he was allowing Megan to get under his skin! She'd been more often in his thoughts than out of them recently.

He'd been tempted to ring Megan and ask how she'd got on the previous night, but thought it might sound as if he was fussing again. He didn't want her to think of him as a bore, or to think he was patronising her. It wasn't always easy to know how to treat women these days. If you were too considerate they seemed to imagine you thought they were brainless idiots, which, if you happened to be naturally polite and thoughtful, could be a drawback.

Megan really was a very independent, confident woman, and had made it clear she didn't need anyone to look after her. So he phoned the hospital instead. There was good news. Mr Jones had broken his collarbone, as Megan had thought, and he also had a minor fracture of his left fibula, but his vertebrae were merely bruised and the spinal cord intact. Naturally he had suffered trauma and, partly because of his age, would need careful monitoring for several days.

Leaving the cottage at a quarter to twelve, Philip drove to Megan's cottage. She opened the door in answer to his knock, already wearing her coat. As she was ready to leave, he made no attempt to enter the house, neither did she invite him in.

'I thought we'd go to a little pub I know on the way to Susan's,' he said, opening the passenger door for her. 'I rang the hospital this morning. They seem to think Mr Jones's condition is stable.'

'Yes, thank goodness,' Megan replied. 'We stayed at the hospital until nearly four this morning. He went into Theatre quickly, thanks to the call you made. I couldn't persuade his wife to leave the hospital until she knew he'd come through the surgery and was in the ward. She seems calmer this morning, after we rang the hospital for news.'

'You mean you stayed with her all night?' Philip glanced at Megan as he got into the driver's seat and started the car. He raised his brows. 'That was good of you, Megan.'

'She was too upset for me to abandon her,' Megan replied with a careless shrug. 'Besides, I've got to know them pretty well since I moved in, and I like them— both of them, but particularly Ellie. She made me feel welcome when I arrived, bringing me tea and offering to help in any way she could. I suppose I felt I should repay her kindness, and she was pretty shaken up by the whole thing. I felt she needed looking after.'

'Well, you've certainly done that,' Philip said, and smiled. 'Had I taken her into Addenbrookes, I would have been forced to leave her there alone. Not that I had any more calls last night.' He saw the signs of strain in Megan's face and frowned. She looked tired, even slightly vulnerable. But she wouldn't thank him for his concern. He had learned that she resented interference.

'I think I probably had more sleep last night than you did.'

'It's lucky I'm not on duty until this evening,' she replied. 'This is my first whole weekend off, so if it was going to happen it was the right moment.'

'It was fortunate you weren't out last night…'

Megan shot a glance at him. Had he betrayed himself by his tone? He knew he resented her intimacy with Robert Crawley, but hoped it didn't show too much.

'I was asked to dinner, as a matter of fact,' Megan said, 'but I turned him down. I like Robert very much as a friend, but I'm not interested in being the next Mrs Crawley so I don't think it's a good idea to make it a regular event. Especially as Robert happens to be looking for a wife rather than a friend.'

Philip wasn't sure why, but he felt ridiculously pleased that she'd turned down Robert Crawley's invitation—and that she didn't want to marry the man.

'It's best to make your position clear from the beginning,' he replied, keeping his tone light and casual. It was clear to him that Megan wanted it that way. 'Friendship is rare between men and women, but it can be very rewarding. Do you agree?'

'Oh, yes, certainly,' she said, her tone and expression giving nothing away. 'As long as the position is clear from the start, no one gets hurt.'

'That's what I've always thought,' Philip said. 'I hope we'll be good friends, Megan.'

'I see no reason why we shouldn't be…'

Philip then asked her if she'd found what she'd wanted in Cambridge, and she said she had, describing some of her purchases in detail. By the time this subject had been exhausted they had reached the sixteenth-century inn Philip had chosen as the venue for their drink.

Over the next half-hour, they talked about the hospital, the village and various upcoming events, their tastes in music, books and films…everything but their personal lives.

Philip thought he knew no more about her, about the real Megan, when he drove her to Susan's than he had earlier in the day. All he did know for certain was that he was finding her more and more attractive, and not just in a physical way.

Susan was eagerly awaiting them. She kissed Phil first and then Megan, complementing her on her trouser suit, which was grey with a thin stripe and worn over a black silk shirt.

'This is lovely,' she said, stroking Megan's sleeves. 'Where did you buy it? Not in Cambridge?'

'No, I found it in London. It was in a sale in Bond Street. I couldn't have afforded it otherwise. It's Escada, and you know their suits cost an arm and a leg, but I got it for half-price,' Megan said. 'Just before I came down, actually. I hadn't bought anything new for ages, not since I went out to Africa. I lived in jeans and T-shirts out there.'

'Yes, I've heard you were out there for a while,' Susan said, so easily that it was obvious she hadn't heard the hospital gossip concerning Megan's reasons for leaving England. 'You were working with children suffering from Aids, weren't you? It must have been heartbreaking, but very worthwhile, of course.'

'Yes, it was.' Megan took a deep breath, obviously realising Susan was going to ask questions and wouldn't be put off by evasion. 'A friend of my sister's found me the job with the project hospital. I had been staying with her for a while to—to get over a disappointment, but I wanted to do something useful and they always need nurses out there. It was a very rewarding job and I loved it. I did think I might stay out there for good, but then I caught malaria quite badly and they told me I would keep on getting it if I stayed there so I decided to come back to England and find a job here. I was still feeling a bit off colour so I thought I might prefer living in the country to the town for a while.'

Philip listened, marvelling at his sister's ability to draw Megan out and wondering why he hadn't managed to get her to talk so easily about herself. His sister seemed to blunder happily in where he himself would have feared to tread.

'I'm so glad you did,' Susan said. 'It is lovely, having you here. We needed a bit of new life in the village. I am sure we'll be good friends. When you have time, I'll take you to some of the regular events and introduce you to everyone.'

'I'd like that...'

The children came out to greet them, but didn't descend on Philip with their usual abandon. They went to hug him, but looked shyly at Megan until she said hello and asked them to tell her whether or not they were going to be in the school concert.

'I've been told all about it,' she said, as everyone went into the comfortable sitting room. 'I understand there's a play and a concert. I hope I'll be able to come, but it depends on whether I'm on duty or not that evening.'

'The concert is next Saturday afternoon,' Jodie piped up. 'I'm singing two songs, aren't I, Mummy?'

'And the play is on Sunday afternoon,' Peter said. 'I'm one of the three kings.'

'Then I must certainly come,' Megan promised. 'I'm on nights that week, so I'll be free in the afternoons.'

After that, Jodie took Megan to look at her doll's

house—a great compliment—and Peter got out his football books.

To Philip's surprise, Megan took it all in her stride. Indeed, she seemed to enjoy being with the children, and by the time dinner was ready she was on the carpet on her knees, helping to build a cut-out cardboard castle Philip had bought for them the previous day.

She was actually very good at finding the right pieces, and Philip lent a hand at the appropriate moment, applying pressure to glue that was difficult to open.

'Phil has such strong hands,' Susan said approvingly. 'He can always open the jars I think are stuck tight. So he's quite handy to have around.'

'Yes, nice hands,' Megan agreed, smiling at what Philip thought of as his sister's attempts to sell him as an eligible partner. 'I would almost have thought a surgeon's hands. Didn't you once think of going in for surgery, Phil?'

'That was before he met Helen,' Susan said without thinking. 'She didn't want him to so...he didn't...' she finished lamely, looking slightly embarrassed. 'Sorry. Don't know what made me bring that up.'

'It doesn't matter. As far as being a surgeon is concerned, I decided it wasn't for me,' Philip replied easily. 'As for the rest, Helen and I were over years ago. Megan knows I'm divorced. I told her.'

'Oh...' Susan looked at him with interest. She knew him too well! For Philip to have told Megan that, he must have thought she was someone special. It was obvious to Philip that his sister was eager to know more about their relationship, but the timer from the cooker saved her from putting her foot in it further and he breathed a sigh of relief. 'Excuse me. That means dinner's ready. Mike, help me dish the vegetables up, please.'

'May I help?' Megan stood up. 'I'd like to, really.'

'Oh…yes, if you like.'

Mike grinned as the two women went out into the kitchen.

'You know Susan's going to put her through the third degree, don't you? If you had any secrets, you won't have by the time they come back. Susan has the Inquisition beaten to a frazzle, believe me. So don't imagine you can hide anything.'

'I didn't,' Philip said, smiling oddly. 'But Megan may have secrets of her own. I hope Susan can take no for an answer. I doubt very much that she's going to hear all she'd like to know. Megan knows how to keep her own counsel.'

'I like her,' Mike said, speaking out more frankly than he normally did. 'I don't know your business, Phil, and don't want to—but she's the right sort. If you're looking for someone to have around for a while, that is?'

Philip nodded. The same thought had been in his mind for a few days now, especially after watching her with the children that morning. It was clear that she'd enjoyed playing with them. It hadn't been put on for his benefit. Megan was far from being just a sexy body, though that couldn't be ignored. Her sense of humour was warm and without malice, and her laughter was infectious. He found her very, very attractive. He just wasn't sure how far either of them wanted the relationship to go.

CHAPTER FOUR

'So, you see, it's quite easy,' Philip said, restoring the tyre he'd removed and tightening the wheel nuts. His demonstration had been offered in a clear, concise manner, making it easy for her to follow. 'But it does take a certain strength. You're probably best going to the garage—or relying on friends to change the wheel in an emergency.'

'I think I could do it if I had to,' Megan replied. 'I'm very grateful to you for showing me, Phil—and for today. I enjoyed myself.' She hesitated, looking at him uncertainly. 'I should ask you in for coffee. Will you think me very rude if I don't? Only I'm on duty this evening. I'm on nights while Sister Riley is off, then I'm back on days again.'

'I understand,' Philip said. 'You want some time to relax before you go on duty. We'll see each other another day. Perhaps dinner when you're free…or the hospital dance. That's on the nineteenth…'

'The dance? I'd heard it mentioned on the grapevine.' Megan looked really pleased to have been asked, but also slightly surprised. 'Yes, I'd love to go with you, Phil. It's good of you to ask me. I wasn't sure what to do about it. I didn't think you went as a rule?'

She must have listened to hospital gossip. Philip knew he was considered a bit of a loner, possibly because he refused to date the nurses.

'I don't,' he said ruefully. 'I always buy tickets, though, because it's for the hospital fund. In the past,

70

I've taken Susan, but she isn't keen on dancing, never has been. She would rather I took the whole family to a pantomime as a treat.'

'Yes, I expect so.' Megan smiled at him. 'She's a mother and thinks of her children first. You have a lovely family, Phil. You're lucky to have them living so close.'

'I bought into the surgery here as a partner for that reason,' he admitted. 'Susan and the children mean a lot to me—Mike, too. I like him and he's good to Susan. She has a lot to do, looking after the terrible two, but we're both available to help if she needs us.'

'She's lucky to have a brother who cares for her,' Megan said, and for a moment Philip caught a wistful note in her voice. He thought he saw a deep sadness in her eyes and wondered what had caused it.

'Do you have any family other than your sister?'

She seemed to hesitate, her eyes taking on what he thought was an oddly bleak expression.

'I have a brother—and my parents are both still alive,' Megan said. 'I don't often see them. I had a disagreement with them some months ago. It's silly really. I should go home and see them...'

'Yes. Best not to let things go on,' Philip said. He moved towards her, hesitated, then reached out to touch her cheek, stroking it with the tips of his fingers. Her skin felt a little warm, almost clammy, and now he thought there was something slightly feverish about her. 'Have you got flu coming on? You look unwell...and you're trembling.'

'It might be a touch of malaria...' Her eyelids fluttered, her gaze shying away from his. 'I think I should go in now, Philip.'

'You should have said you weren't feeling right before,' he said, suddenly anxious. 'Hang on a minute, I'll give you something. I'm sure I have some tablets in my bag.'

'It's all right,' Megan replied. 'Please, don't bother, Phil. I'm used to this. I have the medicine my own doctor prescribed.'

'But you shouldn't be alone—'

'Please, don't fuss!' She cried, then immediately looked apologetic. 'I'm sorry. It's just that I don't feel well…'

'Of course. I'll go. Make sure to call someone if you feel worse, Megan.'

'I shall—thank you for everything.'

Philip watched her go in and shut the door firmly behind her, feeling a twist of regret that the day had ended so abruptly. He'd hoped to stay with her longer, to have a chance to talk to her alone, but she seemed to have erected a barrier beyond which it wasn't permitted to venture.

It wasn't that he wanted to push her into an intimate relationship too soon. He had no wish to frighten her off by trying for too much too soon…which was probably where Crawley had made his mistake.

Philip knew the farmer's reputation. He wasn't a man for letting the grass grow under his feet. He would have made his aspirations very clear. If Megan wasn't prepared to fall into his arms pretty soon, he would look elsewhere.

Philip preferred to take his time, especially where getting to know someone he happened to like quite a lot was concerned. If there was going to be anything more than friendship, it would develop in its own time. He could wait, there was no rush. The rest would come only if she wanted it to happen.

He thought about Megan as he drove home. Her sudden illness was worrying, but bouts of malaria could recur without warning, which was what made it so unpleasant. He would have liked to have made sure she had taken her medicine and seen her safely settled in her home, but he had to trust her judgement. She'd insisted she could cope, and he knew her to be a sensible woman so, despite the way they had parted, he was satisfied with the rate at which their relationship was developing.

Megan had made it clear she wasn't looking for marriage. Well, that was all right. He didn't think he was—though only a few days ago he would have been certain of it!

Now he wasn't quite sure how he felt. Deep inside, there was an almost forgotten hankering to have a family of his own—to experience the warmth of real love.

He was beginning to let himself get too involved! Philip cut the thought off before it could take root. He knew real love was very hard to find. It existed, because Susan and Mike were living proof, but only a few were fortunate enough to find it.

Could he settle for less? Philip considered the options carefully. There was a case for a couple to live together, as friends and lovers, having children because they both wanted a fuller life but without expecting too much.

Or was he dreaming? Wouldn't that sort of arrangement be bound to cause trouble in the end?

Philip spent the remainder of the afternoon tackling a few jobs about the house. The cottage had three bedrooms and had seemed ideal for him when he'd bought it, but if he ever married…

He chuckled to himself. What was he thinking? He went upstairs to take a shower, deciding that he would pop round to see Henry later that evening. There was a practice matter he wanted to discuss. It was time he started thinking about work, instead of filling his mind with foolish dreams...

A busy week followed for Philip. He attended a committee meeting for the hospital fund, took surgery in the mornings and evenings and visited a couple of patients at the hospital in the afternoons. He also phoned Megan twice, but only managed to reach her answering service. She was on nights all week, and was obviously not bothering to respond. However, on the following Monday afternoon, when he was leaving the hospital after visiting his patients, he saw her car in the car park and knew she must be on days again.

He thought about going in search of her, but decided against it. As she hadn't replied to the messages he'd left on her answering machine, it was probably best if he didn't push things for a while. The dinner dance was coming up soon, and he was sure to see her before that.

That evening he drove to the sports club for the squash game he'd arranged with Matthew. He noticed his friend was looking a little flushed, and asked if he felt well enough to play.

'It's the flu coming on, I think,' Matthew said. 'If I'm honest, I don't feel too great, Phil. Would you mind if we just had a drink? After that, I think I'll head home.'

'Of course,' Philip replied. 'Would you like me to prescribe you something? You could stop for it on your way home.'

'Thanks,' Matthew said, 'but I think a couple of aspirins will probably see me through.'

He perched on the edge of his stool as Philip ordered the drinks, but when they arrived made no attempt to touch his own. Philip looked at him in concern. It wasn't like Matthew to ignore a drink, and he was beginning to look very unwell.

'Maybe I should run you home…' Philip suggested.

'Yes, perhaps…'

Matthew stood up, then made a little moaning sound, spun round, clutching at his chest in agony, and collapsed at Philip's feet.

'Matt! Damn!' Philip knelt on the ground beside his friend, feeling for a pulse. Matthew had stopped breathing. 'Matt…'

This wasn't the result of the flu, Philip realised almost instantly. He'd warned Matthew of the dangers of a heart attack several times, but only as a precautionary measure with his future health in mind, never dreaming that an attack had been imminent. He was so stunned that he couldn't believe it.

'He's had a heart attack,' a calm voice said at his side. 'I'll ring for the paramedics. Perhaps you should try giving him CPR, Doctor.'

Megan's crisp, practical tones brought Philip sharply out of his panic attack. He tipped Matthew's head back, made sure the throat was clear with his finger, then started to breathe into his friend's mouth.

He was counting as he began the pumping action that was designed to restart Matthew's heart, only vaguely aware that Megan had made her telephone call and was now kneeling on the floor beside him.

'Let me take over here for a while,' she said. 'Is your bag in the car? You may have something to help him.'

'Yes…yes, I do…' He was so grateful that she was there, with her calm, professional manner and her reassuring voice. 'I'll fetch it…'

Philip had never experienced such terror before. He felt physically sick as he went swiftly out to his car and unlocked it, removing his medical bag. How many times had he used heart massage to resuscitate a patient? Countless! And yet he'd felt like a young student, experiencing his first heart-attack victim. But this was Matthew, and all his years of helping other people through their problems had failed to prepare him for what he was feeling now.

However, by the time he returned to the bar, it was to discover that Matthew's heart had restarted under Megan's competent massage and his eyelids were beginning to flutter open. Philip's professional manner was back in place as he knelt down beside Matthew to administer the injection that could be instrumental in preventing massive damage to the heart muscle.

'It's all right, Matt,' he said as his friend opened his eyes. 'You've had a little bother, but you're going to be fine now. The ambulance will be here soon, and we'll have you in hospital before you know it.'

Matthew's lips moved, though no words came out. His eyes closed again, but his breathing was steady.

'It's all right,' Megan said, her hand on Philip's shoulder. 'He's lucky you were here, Phil. You've probably saved his life.'

'You mean you did,' Philip replied, gazing up at her. 'I'll never be able to thank you enough for what you did—'

'You just needed a jolt,' Megan said. 'When the person dying before your eyes is someone you love, it does give you a jolt. If I hadn't been here, you'd have reacted just the same.'

'Eventually,' Philip agreed. 'I was too stunned to move for a minute.'

'You and thousands of others in the same position.'

'But I'm a doctor. I'm trained for this sort of emergency.'

'So for once you needed some help,' Megan said. 'That doesn't mean you're suddenly a failure, Phil. I think it makes you human.'

The paramedics arrived. Philip was in control as he explained Matthew's condition and what treatment he had given him so far.

'You'll want to go with him,' Megan said as Matthew was lifted onto a stretcher. 'If you trust me to drive your car, I'll follow on with it.'

'Trust you? Yes, of course.' Philip handed over his keys immediately. 'Again, I can't thank you enough—'

'Just go, Phil,' she said. 'I'll see you later.'

Megan returned the keys as Philip sat outside the intensive care ward. He was still feeling stunned by what had happened, and didn't notice her until she came to sit beside him on the hard chairs provided.

'How is he?' she asked, looking at him with sympathy.

'We shan't know for certain for a few hours,' Philip said. 'But they have him under sedation and, as we both know, he'll have a better chance now. He'd be dead if it had happened when he was at home alone.'

Megan nodded. 'Is he a good friend? You seem very fond of him.'

'I suppose Matt is the brother I never had,' Philip replied. 'I've been warning him to lose weight and cut down on his drinking—but I should have made him do it! I should have nagged him into going onto a low-fat diet.'

'It might not have made a difference,' Megan said. 'It could well be stress-related.'

Philip nodded. 'He's been through a rough time of late. His wife left him, and their divorce came through recently. He'd just found someone he liked—'

'Then he'll have something to live for,' Megan said. 'You must try not to worry, Phil. At least Matthew has a chance…'

'Yes, he has a chance,' Philip agreed. He noticed the look of sadness in her eyes, but didn't ask what had caused it. Megan was entitled to her privacy. 'And I can't do anything for him, sitting here. I should go home.'

'Yes, you should,' Megan said. 'And may I, please, beg a lift?'

'Of course.' Philip looked concerned. 'Did you leave your car at the club?'

'No. I went there with a friend this evening. But I need a lift home.'

'My pleasure,' Philip said, his eyes going over her face. 'Are you feeling better?'

'Oh, you mean the other Sunday,' Megan said, dropping her gaze. 'It was nothing. I took my tablets and felt better. I just have to be careful, that's all.'

'I'm glad it was nothing serious,' Philip said. 'Well, we may as well go. I shall telephone in first thing and find out how Matthew is doing.'

'And I'll keep an eye on him,' Megan promised. 'He really is in the best place, Phil.'

'I know.' He smiled at her ruefully. 'You've been terrific, Megan.'

'Thank you.' She laughed as they left the hospital together. 'I think you'll find your car is all in one piece…'

'I'm so sorry,' Susan said when Philip rang her after he got home. 'I had noticed Matthew had put on some weight, but I never expected this. He always seemed so fit.'

'He'd started to show signs of not being fit recently,' Philip said. 'I blame myself, Susan. I should have nagged him into losing weight, although I think Megan was right to suggest that the strain of his divorce played a big part in what happened.'

'Was Megan there with you?'

'She happened to be at the club,' Philip said. 'It was lucky for both of us that she was, Susan. I panicked for a moment. I might have lost valuable time if she hadn't given me a kick up the backside.'

'That doesn't sound like Mr Cool,' Susan said. 'I'm sure you would have coped, Phil, but it must have been a terrible shock for you.'

'Yes, it was,' he replied. 'Matt and I go back a long way.'

'Yes, I know…' She was silent for a moment. 'He mustn't go back to that house of his alone when he comes out, Phil. We have a spare room…'

'I have two,' Philip said. 'I shall certainly offer him the chance to come here, but you know how stubborn he can be.'

'I seem to recall that as a young man he was marginally less stubborn than you, Phil.'

Philip laughed. 'Well, that should stand him in good stead now. As long as he puts up a fight, he should be fine.'

'I am sure he will,' Susan replied. 'Don't worry, love. He has a good chance of recovery.'

'That's what Megan said,' Philip replied. 'I'm sure you're both right.'

He wished his sister goodnight and replaced the re-

ceiver. There really was no point in worrying. He could
do nothing more for the moment except wait.

The news was hopeful the next morning. Matt was holding his own and his doctors were pleased with him.

Philip went to work feeling better than he had all
night. His list was heavy as usual. He gave his patients
his undivided attention, pushing all his personal con-
cerns to the back of his mind. He had a quick lunch at
home, and then a meeting with Lady Rowen about more
fund-raising events.

'We're so lucky to have you, Dr Grant,' she enthused
afterwards. 'It's so seldom we can find anyone who's
willing to devote so much time to helping others.'

'I do what little I can,' Philip replied. 'And now, if
you'll excuse me, I have some hospital visits to make.'

'Of course, of course.' She waved him away with an
arch smile. 'Don't forget I shall be expecting you at my
party, Dr Grant. I know you're always busy, but you
must make time for a little relaxation.'

Philip smiled inwardly as he left her and went out to
his car. Lady Rowen's New Year's Eve party wasn't
exactly a relaxed affair, but she meant well and was
always generous to the hospital.

His first visit at the Chestnuts was to the intensive
care unit. A few words with the sister in charge was
reassuring. All Matthew's vital signs were responding as
they should, and he had regained consciousness that
morning.

'He's still under sedation, Dr Grant,' Sister Rose said.
'I doubt if he'll respond to you because he's very tired,
but he *will* know you're there.'

Philip thanked her. He went to sit by Matthew's bed.
Matthew was surrounded by wires, drips and monitors

that made strange buzzing noises. Philip could imagine how frightening it had to be for relatives who didn't know what all the technology was about. He read Matthew's chart and made all the visual checks for himself—breathing steady, heart response good, blood pressure satisfactory.

'You're doing fine, Matt,' he said, touching his friend's hand. 'Really well. If you keep this up, they'll soon have you out of here.'

Matthew's eyes flicked open and his lips twisted in a lopsided smile. 'Thanks to you…bloody immortals…'

Philip's heart caught. The words were slurred and indistinct, but their meaning was clear enough. Matthew was still there. At the moment his body was unable to respond properly, but his spirit was unbroken.

'Sweet-tempered as usual, I see,' Philip replied in kind. 'Good to see you, Matt. Mustn't stay too long or Sister will be on the rampage. Keep in there, old chap. You'll beat me at squash yet…'

He left Matthew lying there, then went to visit some of his other patients, but when he looked into Megan's office she wasn't around.

Feeling disappointed at not seeing her, Philip drove home. He might try ringing her at the cottage later…

Philip looked out of the hospital window and saw that it was raining again. He frowned, wondering why that fact added to his feeling of being down, and knowing it really had nothing to do with the weather. Several days had passed now since he'd seen Megan, though he knew she'd been at work.

She had left a message on his answerphone one evening. He'd been out on an emergency call at the time.

'Just to say I'm sorry I was out when you rang me,'

Megan had said. 'I've had a lot on recently, Phil. Anyway, I just wanted to say that I'm so glad Matthew is doing well. I went to see him, and they told me they were going to move him out of Intensive Care. If I don't hear from you before then, I presume you'll pick me up on the nineteenth…'

It was purely and simply because Philip wanted to see her that he made his way to the medical ward that afternoon. He had already visited Matthew, who was sitting up in bed and looking as if he was enjoying all the attention from several pretty nurses.

'This is the life,' Matthew had said with his usual wicked grin. 'I think I took up the wrong profession, Phil. I should have joined the immortals. You're spoilt for choice.'

'Just remember you're in here to rest,' Philip remarked wryly. 'I see I can stop worrying about you.'

After leaving Matthew, he visited Mr Jones, the patient who had fallen down stairs a week or so earlier.

Mr Jones had been transferred from Addenbrookes earlier that day. Apart from feeling a little tired after the transfer, the elderly man was making good progress. His pain was being managed, and he seemed to have come through the incident remarkably well. There was still the problem of what had caused the accident in the first place, of course, but Mrs Jones blamed a pair of worn-out slippers. CT scans had shown that there was no new scarring of the brain, and Philip was fairly sure that Mr Jones hadn't suffered a stroke—there was certainly no evidence of clogging or a blood vessel bursting in the brain, which was a good sign. So perhaps the slippers were to blame. It wouldn't be the first time worn slippers had caused a nasty fall.

Philip was thoughtful as he reached Megan's office.

He might just ask her what she thought about some counselling for the couple, who were approaching the time when they might need outside help.

Megan's door was closed so he knocked once and then opened it in case she was out on her rounds. She was standing with her back towards him, her hand resting on the telephone as if she had just replaced the receiver. Something about the set of her shoulders started mental alarm bells ringing.

'Megan…' he said hesitantly. 'Is something wrong?'

She turned to face him and he saw that her lovely green eyes were drenched with tears. She was clearly struggling to contain her emotion but finding it impossible to disguise her distress.

He moved towards her, reaching out impulsively to gather her into his arms, holding her tenderly and with great care, as if she were so fragile she might crumble. He ran his fingers over her hair, then stroked the back of her neck. She tensed for a mere fraction of a second, then went limp and allowed him to hold her, her head against his shoulder as the tears simply flowed.

It was a short but very emotional outburst. She wept frantically for a minute or so, then shuddered, taking a deep breath as she fought to recover her composure.

Philip took out his handkerchief to wipe her cheeks. His ministrations were gentle, and after a moment she glanced up at his concerned face and gave him a tremulous smile. He felt a sharp charge of desire, a need to hold her again—as much for his own comfort as hers. Before he knew what he was doing he had drawn her back to him, losing his fingers in her hair and tipping her head towards him.

Her mouth was soft and inviting beneath his, just as he had imagined it. He felt her respond, her body so soft and warm that it seemed to melt into his, the seductive fragrance of her freshly washed hair filling his senses.

She felt so good close to him, just as he'd instinctively known she would. His kiss deepened, becoming much more than the gentle, comforting caress he'd intended, arousing his body in a way it hadn't been in a long, long time. He wanted her badly, wanted to hold her like this for ever.

Megan's response was equally passionate. She clung to him as though her life depended on him holding her. He was surprised at her reluctance to let him go when he released her after that kiss, but he had to do it. Now was not the time or place for the feelings he was experiencing.

Megan seemed to have calmed down. She took the handkerchief he had used earlier to wipe her tears and blew her nose, then pocketed it with a watery laugh.

'I've put lipstick all over your handkerchief. Sorry, I'll give it back to you when I've washed it. What an idiot I am,' she said, slightly flushed. 'Sorry about all the drama. It was just…that I'd received some bad news. A telephone call…'

'Just before I came in?' She nodded and he frowned, realising his unexpected arrival had probably provoked her tears. 'You would rather have been quiet, I expect. I shouldn't have intruded without your permission. Forgive me, please. Shall I go—or would you like to talk about it?'

'Simon…has just died,' Megan said in a choking voice. 'It was expected. He had been suffering from a malignant lymphoma. He was ill for some time before he sought treatment, by which time…' She shrugged her shoulders, swallowing a sob. 'He underwent a course of chemotherapy, which seemed to help for a time, but it

had gone too far and…he finally lost the fight a couple
of hours ago. A friend who works at the hospice he was
in just rang to give me the news.'

'Simon—he was someone you cared for?'

'Simon was—*is* my brother,' Megan said, her eyes
reproaching him. Her voice was hoarse with distress as
she went on, 'It was *his* wedding… You wouldn't come
and it meant so much to me. Simon and I were so
close…'

'Oh, Megan,' Philip said, horrified that he could have
been so insensitive. 'I didn't realise… Your brother
Simon. Yes, of course, I do remember now you've reminded me.'

'No, you don't,' Megan said. 'You didn't even remember I had a brother. You asked me if I had any
family the other day after we went to your sister's. It
upset me, made me remember how ill…'

Philip was stricken with remorse. 'It happened such a
long time ago, but I ought to have remembered. I should
have known you had a brother. Please, forgive me.'

'Why should you have remembered? We were only
friends—there was nothing serious between us.'

'We were more than that,' he replied. 'Even if I was
such an arrogant fool that I didn't realise it until it was
too late.'

Megan nodded, as if accepting what he'd said. 'I've
wanted to tell you,' she went on. 'I've been so worried
about Simon. I almost told you the night Matthew was
taken ill. You seemed more approachable that night—as
if you could feel pain like the rest of us.'

'And I don't usually seem that way to you?'

'Not always,' she admitted. 'You do have a way of
keeping people at a distance, Phil. You always did—'

'Not you, Megan. I've never meant to keep you at a

distance. And I am very sorry about your brother,' Philip said gently, his manner much the same as that he showed to the families of terminally ill patients. But his heart wrenched for her pain, and he knew he was more involved than he'd realised until that moment. 'You were obviously very fond of him.'

'Yes. We were always close, especially after…' She shook her head and let out a sobbing breath. 'But, as I said, it was expected. I don't know why it affected me like that all of a sudden. I'm sorry for being so silly.' Her head went up, her expression becoming that of a professional nurse. 'You wanted to see me. Was it a medical matter?'

'Yes,' Philip said, then hesitated. He wanted a lot more than that but her emotional outburst had put him off balance. 'Yes and no. I did want to talk about Mr and Mrs Jones, to see what you thought about getting the welfare people involved, but I also wanted to speak to you on a personal level. I wondered if you'd like to come out with me this evening? Dinner or a film perhaps? I believe there's quite a decent one on, a romantic comedy, *Shakespeare in Love*? But perhaps you don't feel like going out?'

'I think it would be better than staying in alone,' she said. 'I'll go home tomorrow, of course, but for this evening… And the film you mentioned sounds good. I had noticed it was showing again. I've wanted to see it for ages,' Megan said. 'I wouldn't mind seeing it, but are you sure you want to? I wouldn't have thought of you as the romantic type.'

Philip was pleased to see the humour back in her eyes. She was truly an amazing woman, he thought. Her life had been touched by tragedy, but if he hadn't happened to have caught her at a weak moment he might never have known it. She was a very strong person. He admired her bravery, and found himself wanting to protect her, to bring the laughter back to her lovely eyes.

He raised his brows, giving her a quizzical look. 'You *have* been listening to the hospital grapevine. Tell me, what do the hospital gossips have me down as—a boring GP or a misogynist?'

Megan chuckled. The sound was warm and husky, and he found it very appealing, especially as he knew that underneath she was fighting her grief.

'Neither, actually,' she said, then shook her head. 'No, I'm not going to tell you. All I'll say is that you've set a lot of hearts fluttering in these hallowed halls, Phil.'

He pulled a wry face. 'No accounting for what goes on in the minds of women!'

'Oh, I think there is in some of them,' Megan replied. 'According to one of our staff nurses, you're tall, dark and entirely edible.'

'You mean Anne Browne, of course,' Philip remarked in a resigned tone that drew a laugh but no confirmation. 'Anne seems to think of half the male staff in that way.'

'But you aren't interested?' Megan arched her brows teasingly.

'A nice girl, but not my type.'

Megan nodded, making no further comment. 'Will you pick me up this evening?'

'Yes. For once I'm not taking evening surgery. Shall we say seven at your cottage?'

'Thank you. I'll be ready.' She looked at him a little anxiously. 'I'm sure I don't have to ask, but you won't mention what I told you just now to anyone, will you?'

'No, most certainly not,' Philip said. 'I'm not one of the hospital gossips.' He was slightly offended that she'd even thought it necessary to ask, but did his best to hide it. 'I'll see you this evening. I'm taking surgery only from three until five, then Henry takes over.'

He smiled at her and left, aware of mixed emotions.

Her response to his kiss had surprised him, but he'd sensed it had been because she'd been overwrought. Had he not entered her office until some minutes later, when she had mastered her feelings of shock and grief, she would quite possibly have been her usual self.

CHAPTER FIVE

PHILIP sensed that his patient was frightened by the news he had just given her. She was still young to be facing the prospect of having a hysterectomy. Although she already had a child, she had possibly hoped to have more one day.

'It's not the operation itself that worries me,' she explained as Philip tried to reassure her. 'I would need so much time off work, and I can't possibly afford it. We have commitments—I *need* to work.'

Philip nodded, understanding her problem. 'You ought to think seriously about having this done, Mrs Jackson,' he said, and paused. 'I've heard about a surgeon who's pioneering keyhole hysterectomies. If I could arrange it—and at this stage I can't promise anything—would you be prepared to go ahead?'

'What difference would it make?'

'You would be in hospital no more than a day and a half, and would probably be back at work within a month. Much better than the average three months, I think you will agree?'

'Is it more dangerous?'

'I would say possibly less so,' Philip said, looking thoughtful. 'There's less chance of the blood clotting this way. The operation takes ninety minutes rather than sixty, and there's less pain afterwards and less scarring of the tissues.'

'It does sound easier, but I would still like to think

about it,' Mrs Jackson said. 'Can I talk to my husband and my boss and come back to you?'

'Yes, of course. It must be your own decision.' He smiled at her. 'Meanwhile, I'll do more research and see if it would be possible to get you in. I expect there's a huge waiting list.'

After she'd gone, Philip finished entering her notes on the computer, then picked up his briefcase and left his consulting room.

'You're off early today, Dr Grant.'

'Yes. I'm going out this evening.' He smiled at the receptionist. 'Following your advice, Mrs Brodie.'

'That's right, Doctor. You should have more time for yourself.'

Philip was thoughtful as he drove home. He was looking forward to being with Megan that evening, but not clear where they were going emotionally. She seemed to give out different signals. At one moment she was a warm, melting body in his arms, a woman who he suspected, was very sexually aware, very loving and giving, and at other times she seemed to become someone different, cool, slightly reserved, as if retreating behind a barrier.

To prevent herself getting hurt? Philip could understand that, because he knew from experience how it felt when someone was left feeling battered and bruised after an emotional disruption. It made one afraid to give anything ever again.

Philip would never want to hurt Megan. He respected and liked her too much to cause her pain, though he was still not certain how far he wanted this relationship to progress. However, he did know that she was often on his mind.

He also knew that he badly wanted to make love with her.

* * *

'I'm glad you enjoyed the film.' Philip smiled at Megan as she fastened her seat belt. 'Are you hungry? Would you like to stop for something to eat before we go home?'

'We could have a snack at my cottage,' Megan said at once. 'Just something light, something that won't keep either of us awake. If that suits you?'

'That sounds good to me.'

He glanced at her as he started the car. Was he imagining things or had she become quieter as the evening progressed? She'd laughed during the film, seeming to lose herself in the slightly zany plot, and had apparently enjoyed the chocolate toffees and popcorn they'd shared. Once or twice she had touched his arm, even holding his hand as they'd communicated their amusement at various events in the film.

Philip had liked it that they found the same things funny. Sometimes it almost felt as if he'd known her for years, as if, after a long journey in a dark, lonely place, he had suddenly found his way home.

Once or twice he'd found himself watching her instead of the film, wondering what would have happened if he'd gone to her brother's wedding with her all those years ago.

Philip hadn't made a move on her. He was way past the stage of using a darkened cinema for furthering a love affair. There were better places for kissing, but that didn't mean he wasn't very aware of her sitting beside him in the darkness. It didn't stop him appreciating the soft, seductive perfume that wafted towards him when she moved—or the desire he felt.

Had he been a few years younger, less cautious, less afraid of bruising her feelings, Philip might have followed the example of the ardent teenage couple a few seats away, but he managed to restrain himself.

Megan herself was probably unaware of how attractive he found her. At least, he hoped he was putting up a good show of offering a simple friendship with no strings attached even if he had slipped up when he'd kissed her. Just because sexual relationships were ten a penny these days, that didn't mean a woman had to fall into bed every time she was asked.

Neither of them spoke much on the drive back to the village. Perhaps Megan was merely being considerate, understanding that he needed to give his full attention to the road. Conditions were quite treacherous in places. An icy mist hung over the surrounding countryside, making it difficult to see more than a few yards ahead, and the road was slippery.

When they reached Megan's cottage she went on ahead, switching on lights, bringing the place alive with warmth and colour. She had banked up the coal fire before she'd left, and it was still glowing, giving out a pleasant heat behind the wire screen.

Philip knew the cottage had been rented furnished, but it was easy to see where Megan had added homely touches of her own, with displays of foliage and flowers, bright ethnic throws on the settee and photographs in all kinds of different frames, from a silver one to another decorated with teddy bears.

While she went to switch on the coffee-machine Philip wandered about the sitting room, looking at her books, CDs and photos. Most of them seemed to be of a woman who looked as if she might be Megan's sister, a man who was probably her husband and three rather attractive children.

'That's Beth, Arnie and the kids,' Megan said when she came back to see him holding a family picture. 'The oldest boy is Richard, then there's Lizzy and Mark. In her last letter Beth told me she's expecting another baby in the spring.'

He couldn't see a photograph of anyone who might have been her brother or of a man who might be important in her life. Perhaps she found it too painful to have pictures of Simon around at the moment.

'Susan tells me she wants at least another two. We've always been quite close.'

Megan nodded. 'I've always been close to Beth, as well as my brother. I think it's because our parents were always so busy. They both had careers that were important to them, and we had various nannies while we were growing up. It wasn't that our parents didn't love us, just that they expected us to be adult about things before we were ready.'

'I suppose it was a bit that way for Susan and me,' Philip said after a moment's thought. 'We lost our mother when we were teenagers. Father died just last year. I still miss him—'

His thoughts were interrupted by a pinging sound from the kitchen.

'Coffee and toasted sandwiches,' Megan explained. 'With you in a couple of minutes.'

Philip nodded, watching her walk away. He'd noticed before how fascinating her walk was, but he wasn't thinking about making love to her at that moment. This was the first time he and Megan had really talked about things that mattered, apart from her emotional outburst earlier that afternoon, which was a very different thing.

She was obviously opening up to him a little, beginning to trust him.

He would have liked to have tried taking their relationship a little further, but knew he had to be careful. He didn't want to spoil things by pushing too much.

Megan returned in a few minutes with a tray. She had made a plate of sandwiches in a special toaster similar to one Philip owned, the fillings tasty and light. He ate three, noticing she hardly touched even her coffee as they discussed the options for Mr and Mrs Jones.

'There's a small amount of old scarring shown on the CT scan,' Philip told Megan. 'I think he may have had a slight stroke, without realising it, some time ago. As you know, it happens that way quite often. After that fall, I'm uneasy about leaving them to get on with things just in case he is beginning to fail. How do you think they would feel about the offer of help from social services?'

'She might be pleased—he would resent it,' Megan said without hesitation. 'I'll have a word if you like, tell her what the various options would mean for them both, see if she's interested in talking to someone for her own sake. But I wouldn't do anything official just yet if I were you. Mr Jones is very independent.'

'I'll leave it to you, then.' Philip smiled at her, then glanced at his watch. It was getting late. He stood up, feeling reluctant yet knowing he had to leave. He wanted Megan, wanted her so badly it was like an ache inside him, but it would be wrong to put his own desires before her needs. He wasn't selfish or greedy enough to prey on her while she was vulnerable. 'Well, I suppose I ought to be—'

Megan was reaching for the cream jug. He noticed her hand shaking, saw the accident in the making as she jerked and sent the jug flying, spilling cream all over the tray, and heard her gasp of dismay. She looked pale, tense. All at once he knew he hadn't been mistaken in the car. She was struggling against her feelings.

'Megan?' He moved towards her. It was obvious that she was fighting her emotions. Any other woman might have been in tears by now, but she wouldn't let go, hanging onto her emotions by a thin thread. 'What is it? Is it because of Simon? Can I help?'

'Please…' Megan raised her head, looking at him with eyes that pleaded for understanding. 'Philip…I can't be alone tonight. I've been fighting this all evening…' She took a sobbing breath but still no tears fell. 'I know I have no right to ask this…but will you stay? Will you be with me?' There was a faint flush in her cheeks now, but she continued bravely. 'You kissed me this afternoon. Would you…? Could you…?'

Philip moved swiftly towards her. He understood one thing. Megan needed him, wanted him, and he'd been a damned fool to hesitate. There was a time for caution, and a time when thinking too much was dangerous.

'Hush,' he murmured as he reached out for her, taking her to him, holding her. 'No need to ask, love. I've been wanting this from the first moment I saw you.'

He bent his head to kiss her. Her mouth was soft and warm beneath his, responding with an urgency that matched his own. He knew that she needed this, needed the warmth of touching another person, of being close to someone, and that this chemistry had been there between them from the very beginning.

It wasn't just because she was so desperately unhappy. She felt she could trust him, needed him to help her through this in a special way. Megan was a warm, passionate woman, and making love with a man who cared would be a healing process for her.

Philip was a gentle man, a considerate man. Loving for him—making love—was always a two-way thing. He needed to give pleasure as much as to take it for himself. This time it was more important than ever. Megan's feelings were all that mattered. He wanted to give her the comfort, the release he knew she needed, the ease from emotional tension that only physical contact gave. And he wanted to make her laugh, because with laughter came confidence.

'Do you know, the first time I saw you at the Chestunuts I couldn't take my eyes off your legs,' he murmured teasingly against her ear. 'I think you must be the best tonic the men's ward can get. And that walk of yours has been keeping me awake for the past week.'

Megan laughed, her body melding to his as their kiss deepened and intensified. It was as if an electric cable had switched on, had somehow made them tinglingly alive. Suddenly they were both eager, almost desperate, in their need, clinging to each other, hands reaching, touching, mouths searching, hot and greedy in their hunger.

Philip could no longer even claim to be thinking. He was hardly able to control his shuddering as they helped each other to undress. Neither of them seemed able to manage his shirt buttons, and in a frenzy of impatience he ripped away the last two as he tore it open.

Megan chuckled. Her sweater was much more simple to deal with—one fluid, swooping movement and it lay with his ruined shirt on the sitting-room carpet. Zips were much easier to overcome and somehow, despite their clumsiness, they managed to dispose of the unwanted barriers to their passion until both were naked and lying on the accommodating vastness of the old sofa.

'You're so beautiful,' he breathed in reverent tones. 'Really lovely, and so nice to touch.'

For a moment he hardly dared to touch her, but his eyes feasted on her flesh—such lovely, full breasts, the nipples taut like sweet, dark rosebuds, telling him, had he needed to be told, that she was already aroused. Her skin was a soft cream, silky smooth beneath his fingers as he reached for her, his thumb caressing her breast seconds before his mouth sucked gently at the nipple.

'Philip...' Megan's voice was husky, caught with emotion. 'I...'

'Yes?' He raised his head to look at her, needing no words to tell him what was in her mind. 'I know, my love, I know...'

'Please...' She pressed herself against him. 'Please, love me. Just for tonight...'

'Who could help loving you?' Philip held her close, his hands stroking the length of her back, cupping her firm bottom, pressing her against him so that his hungry need, his own desire, had to be more than evident to her. 'You're a lovely woman, Megan. Not just your body, but you—all of you.'

His first desperate need to touch her had eased now. He was in control of his physical movements, determined that his own desire would not be allowed to spoil this first love-making. He wanted to make it special for her, to take away the pain he suspected she had held inside for far too long.

And it was so good just to hold her, to inhale the perfume of her skin, to feel her, to feel her against him. He wanted to know every part of her, to stroke the softness of her inner thighs, to taste her with his tongue and lips.

Only when she was sighing and trembling with the force of her own desire, when she called his name so urgently that he knew she needed him inside her, did he allow himself to thrust deep into her welcoming warmth.

It was like music, the tumultuous throb and swell of a fine orchestra slowly building to a wondrous crescendo. Philip experienced a kind of pleasure he had never felt before. He was aware of something inside him as they moved together, something that transcended the purely physical act. It filled him, filled his senses, engulfed him like a tide of rushing water, but warm water, sweet, comforting and fierce at the same time. His throat was tight, his breathing harsh, croaky, as he whispered her name over and over.

He was aware of a great tenderness as he gathered Megan against him after their passion was spent. It felt right somehow, the way their bodies fitted together. He stroked her hair, aware that her cheeks were damp, though he doubted whether she knew she had wept as they'd reached that far, beautiful place together. She wasn't a woman for tears, though he was pretty damned near them himself.

After a few moments Philip realised that Megan was sleeping. He glanced down at her. She looked so peaceful that there was no way he was going to wake her. He reached up for the throw that hung over the back of the sofa. It was soft and warm to the touch, and would cover them both sufficiently should the fire go out.

Philip closed his eyes. When he opened them again, he found he was alone on the settee. He sat up gingerly, aware of a crick in his neck. The old chesterfield was fine for napping, but not the most comfortable bed in the world.

It must be almost dawn, he realised. At some time during the night the fire had gone out, but Megan had switched on an electric one. Her clothes had disappeared, and he could smell coffee brewing. She must have woken earlier and left him sleeping. He knew she must be getting ready to leave. She probably wanted to catch an early train.

He picked up his clothes and dressed, shaking his head wryly at the ripped shirt. His cleaning lady would wonder what had happened when she came to iron it the next time. He was just putting on his jacket when Megan brought a mug of coffee through. She set it on the table next to him.

He was aware of the tension in her, of her attempts to hide it from him, and was silent as he reached for the coffee-mug.

'Can you let yourself out?' she asked, not quite looking at him.

He wondered if she was embarrassed or regretting what had happened.

Philip brought himself up sharply, knowing that it was an awkward situation and that he ought to do something about it, yet somehow not able to take it in his stride because he was afraid it might mean quite a lot to him.

'Yes, of course.'

'I need to get a shower and—'

'Yes, I know,' he said. 'I'll drink this and go. You have to get off. Don't worry about me. Let me know when you come back...'

'Yes...' She hesitated. 'Phil...'

'Thank you for last night,' he said as she was unable to continue. 'You're not angry with me?'

'Of course not. Why should I be?'

'Just wondered.' He drank some of the coffee and set the mug down. 'I ought to go. I'll be in touch soon. I'll ring you in the week, Megan.'

'Yes, do that,' she said. 'Excuse me, I have to get ready.'

'Yes, of course.' He hesitated, not liking to leave it this way but aware that neither of them seemed able to behave naturally. 'Don't forget the hospital dance…'

Megan nodded, then turned and walked away from him.

Philip let her go, watching as she disappeared into the kitchen. For a moment he was tempted to go after her, to say something that would make her smile, to make her as she had been the previous evening, but he couldn't. He wasn't sure quite what to say, what she expected of him. Neither was he certain of his own feelings about all this. What had happened hadn't been just a one-night stand, at least not on his side. He couldn't think of it like that—it had been too special.

So what exactly had happened between them?

There was an emotional involvement here. Philip acknowledged the truth to himself as he drove back to his cottage. The chemistry between them was strong and couldn't be denied, but was it just going to turn into an affair—or something that might last longer?

He would be seeing Megan when he took her to the hospital's Christmas dance, which was being held the following weekend. Perhaps he would stand back for a few days, let them both have a chance to think things through.

Philip glanced through the post on his desk at the surgery. Besides some results from the hospital labs, there was the usual assortment of literature from pharmaceutical companies, an interesting circular about a course open to general practitioners and their staff and his copy of the *British Medical Journal*. He flicked through the magazine, noting one or two articles he would read later, then picked up a pile of patients' notes and looked through them.

One of his first patients that Thursday morning was a child who had just been diagnosed as having leukaemia. There was no easy way to break the news to Carol's mother. At four years old, the child herself would hardly understand what was happening. She just knew she felt tired and ill and disliked being pulled about by the doctors.

Philip thought of all the uncomfortable treatment and difficult days ahead for Carol and her parents, and decided it was best to have them in immediately, even though they were actually third on his list.

As soon as Carol and her mother came in, Philip could tell that Mrs Bond suspected the worst.

'It's cancer, isn't it?' she said. 'She has sore places in her mouth now, Doctor.' Her eyes were wide and scared. 'I'm going to lose her, aren't I?'

Philip turned to the child with a reassuring gesture. 'Let me have a look inside your mouth, please, Carol.'

He made a brief inspection, then buzzed for the practice nurse. In the meantime, he smiled at the little girl and gave her a sweet from the dish on his desk.

'Nurse Jill is going to take you away and show you some new toys,' he said. 'Be a good girl, Carol, and Mummy won't be long.'

'She's going to die, isn't she?' Mrs Bond burst into tears as soon as the door closed behind her daughter and the nurse. 'I know it, so don't lie to me.'

'I'm not going to lie to you,' Philip said. 'I asked you to come in this morning because we have had the results of those tests now. Carol has leukaemia, as we suspected. It's a disease, as I'm sure you know, in which the blood contains an abnormally large number of white blood cells. It's a form of cancer of the blood-forming tissues, which undergo uncontrolled proliferation and...' He saw that Mrs Bond's eyes were glazed, fixed. She was too distressed to take any of this in right now. 'It means Carol is very ill,' he said gently, 'but the disease can often be controlled these days.'

'How?' she demanded. 'What are they going to do to my baby?'

'She'll be treated either by radiotherapy or cytotoxic drugs.'

'Does that mean her hair will fall out and she'll be sick all the time?'

'It isn't going to be easy,' Philip said. 'I can't pretend that we can make Carol better overnight.'

'But she's so little...' Tears filled the mother's eyes.

'Your daughter will go into hospital for the treatment I described. Everything possible will be done for her, Mrs Bond. I'll make all the arrangements myself, and I'm going to make sure Carol gets specialist treatment at an excellent children's unit. The specialist will be able to tell you exactly what Carol needs then. All I would say to you now is that you mustn't give up hope. There is hope, Mrs Bond. I believe we've got in early in Carol's case, and that's always good news. Believe me, they can do much more for her than was the case a few years ago. There are never any guarantees, but I personally think she has a good chance of stabilising her condition.'

She nodded, wiping the tears from her eyes with a

tissue from a box he offered. 'She's our only child. My husband works so hard for us. He wouldn't come with me this morning. He can't bear the idea that she might have—'

'I'll call round this evening and have a chat with him, bring some leaflets he might like to read,' Philip said. 'Try not to let yourself get too distressed, Mrs Bond. Carol needs you. She's more important than your own feelings just now. Be brave for her.'

'Yes. I will try.' Her head went up. 'Thank you for your patience, Dr Grant. I feel better now.'

Philip took her hand for a moment before she left. 'Sometimes counselling helps. I'll arrange for a visitor. We're all here to help you, Mrs Bond. If you need us, don't hesitate to ask.'

He sat staring at the door as it closed behind her. It was true that there was hope for Carol, especially as he believed the disease was in its early stages, but he understood the mother's despair. He could imagine what he would have felt like if it had been Jodie or Peter who had developed the disease.

Philip stood up and went to stare out of the window for a moment. Sometimes it was a foul job! He knew a feeling of hopelessness. What good was all his training, all his dedication, when all he had to give Mrs Bond were meaningless words?

He closed his eyes for a moment, and the memory of a woman's soft, yielding body came unbidden into his mind. Megan. The name was like a cooling breath of air on a summer's day to his senses. He felt the longing stir inside him and knew he wanted her—not just sexually, but to talk with, to share his thoughts. She would understand…

Philip laughed suddenly, shaking off his mood.

Perhaps he would see Megan later when he visited the hospital.

He went back to his desk, then realised his next patient was Jennifer Russell and buzzed for her. She came into the room and he saw she was smiling.

'What can I do for you, young lady? Is your foot giving you pain?' He glanced down and saw that she was wearing her special trainers. He hoped that he hadn't been mistaken in buying them for her.

'There's nothing wrong with me,' said Jennifer, dismissing with characteristic cheerfulness the ache in her back which he knew, never quite left her despite her pills and all the treatment. She placed a small box of chocolates on his desk. 'Mum sent these to say thanks for all you did for me. And I've come to ask you a special favour...'

'Oh, and what's that?'

The twinkle was back in Philip's eyes as she twiddled a strand of hair around her finger. Young Jennifer had her own special charm! She was after something.

'We need someone to be Father Christmas at the Hospital Supporters children's party,' Jennifer said. 'Mr Jones was going to do it, but he had a fall. I suggested you, but everyone said it wasn't fair to ask because you were so busy.'

'When is the party?'

'This Sunday afternoon at four.' Jennifer looked at him guiltily. 'Mum doesn't know I've asked. She thinks I came because of this...' She pointed to a little cold sore on her chin.

Philip looked at the spot. 'I'll give you a prescription for some cream. Nothing to worry about, young lady. And you can tell your friends I shall be delighted to help out—just this once. I'll telephone the organisers and arrange to come along in plenty of time.'

'I knew you would,' Jennifer said, clearly delighted at her success.

'Then stop wasting my valuable time, and let me get on,' Philip replied, but with a smile that sent her on her way with a giggle.

Philip didn't know about Jennifer, but her visit had been just the tonic he'd needed! Thinking about all the suffering Jennifer had endured, in and out of hospital so many times over the years, her courage and constant good humour despite so many operations, it made Philip remember just why he was a doctor.

He wasn't omnipotent. He couldn't make everyone better by waving a magic wand, but sometimes he could do a little to help someone and that was what it was all about.

The telephone was ringing when Philip walked into the cottage. He snatched it up eagerly. 'Megan?'

'No, it's Susan,' his sister said. 'I was just ringing to see where you've been. We haven't seen you for ages. The kids were asking if you'd moved.'

'Sorry,' Philip apologised. 'I've been busy. When I get an hour or so to spare I pop in to see Matt—but I'll try to get round soon.'

'How is Matthew?'

'Much better…getting impatient. He wants to run before he can walk. He keeps nagging me to get the doctors to let him out, but I've told him it isn't up to me.'

'And now I'm nagging you,' Susan said, and laughed. 'I'm sorry, Phil. You will come for Christmas Day, won't you—and bring Megan?'

'I'm seeing her soon,' Philip replied. 'I'll ask her. I

hadn't realised how near it was getting. The time goes so fast, and it just seems to creep up on me. I still haven't fixed myself up for Lady Rowen's party.'

'But you'll take Megan, of course,' his sister said, sounding puzzled. 'I'm sure she'd like to go, and if you ask her in time she can change duties if she needs to. Wake up, Phil! Megan Hastings is the best thing that's happened to you in years.'

Susan rang off before he could reply.

Philip frowned as he drew into the hospital car park. He'd deliberately not phoned Megan for a couple of days because he'd needed time to think, but in his heart he knew that it was too late to draw back. He was already involved—and he wanted it that way!

As he got out of the car he saw Megan coming towards him. She was just taking her car keys from her bag, and she seemed to hesitate as she saw him. Usually so cool and in control, she looked flustered, unsure of what to say.

'How are you?'

'Better—thank you.'

'I'm glad we've met like this,' Philip said, smiling at her. 'I just wanted to apologise for not ringing, as I promised. I've been busy, but I should have made a quick call. Will you forgive me?'

'Yes, of course...' She glanced down at the ground. 'It's me who should apologise for taking advantage of your good nature.' Her eyes swept up to his then. 'I know it doesn't mean anything, Phil. I'm not expecting anything. You only stayed because I asked.'

'If I hadn't wanted to, you could have begged on your knees and it wouldn't have made any difference,' Philip said in a bantering tone that brought an immediate laugh.

'Good grief, Megan! You can't imagine that I was doing you a favour? If anything, it would be the other way round—but I rather thought it was nice for both of us.'

'Yes, of course,' she said, relaxing now. 'Very nice.'

'Nice enough to repeat?' He was tense as he waited for her reply, which seemed an age in coming and made him wonder if he'd pushed her too far.

'I…see no reason why not.' Megan's head went up, her eyes meeting his on a direct level, challenging him. 'We're both old enough to know our own minds, aren't we? Neither of us is going to make demands on the other. It isn't as if either of us is looking for marriage, or even a settled relationship.'

'I hope it won't be too transient,' Philip said, giving her a mischievous look that brought another laugh. 'I like having you around, Megan. And before it slips my mind again, I'd like you to keep Christmas Day and New Year's Eve free…if you can? I know that's being a bit greedy, but if you don't ask you don't get.' He grinned at her and was rewarded by a smile.

'Yes, as it happens, I'm free for both,' Megan replied. 'I'm working on Christmas Eve and New Year's Day because a colleague asked if we could do it that way…so, yes, I can keep those dates free. Had you something particular in mind?'

'Sorry!' Philip laughed at himself. 'I'm expecting you to read my mind now. There's an important party on New Year's Eve at Lady Rowen's house—business really. If I'm very nice to her, she may give us a really large cheque for the fund. Christmas Day is at Susan's— a proper family thing with a tree and presents, far too much food and the Queen's address to the nation. We can slip away after that if we like. Susan was on to me about bringing you a few minutes ago, actually, but I'd intended to ask anyway.'

'Sounds lovely,' Megan said, looking pleased with the idea. 'And, of course, I shall see you tomorrow evening for the dance.'

Philip nodded. He hesitated, a gleam of mischief in his eyes. 'Could you spare an hour on Sunday afternoon?'

'I am off this weekend,' Megan said, an answering amusement in her own eyes. 'You're up to something, Phil. I can see it in your face. What have you done now?'

'I don't know quite how it happened,' he replied, 'but I've promised Jennifer Russell that I'll be Father Christmas at the children's party this weekend.'

'This I shall move heaven and earth to see!' Megan declared wickedly. 'How did she manage to persuade you, Phil—put a gun to your head?'

'She caught me at a weak moment,' he said, and then, without breaking patient confidentiality, found himself telling Megan about Carol Bond and the way he'd given into a moment of despair after speaking to her distraught mother.

'You're too nice,' Megan said, and moved impulsively to kiss his cheek. 'I'd have thought after all these years you'd have begun to harden yourself to these things.'

'Have you?' He resisted the temptation to kiss her in a very different manner.

She smiled oddly and shook her head. 'No, but I thought I was the only one who was that much of an idiot. We're professionals, Phil. We're not supposed to have feelings, but I can't help it sometimes.'

'Now you know there are at least two of us,' Philip

said. He shook his head at his own thoughts. 'I'm back on course now. So, where are you going this afternoon?'

'I have a couple of hours I've managed to swop with a colleague,' Megan said. 'I wanted to pop into Cambridge and finish my Christmas shopping. I shan't have another opportunity.'

'I've got some more things to buy,' Philip said, looking thoughtful. 'It's almost here, isn't it? I'll have to see if I can get in myself in the morning or I shan't manage it either.'

'I must go,' Megan apologised. 'I've only got a couple of hours.'

'I'll pick you up on Saturday,' he said. 'Don't let me hold you up. I have a couple of visits to make, then it's back to the surgery. I'm doing both the afternoon and the evening duties today.'

Philip watched as she got into her car and drove away. He wasn't quite sure how he felt about their conversation. Megan was happy to continue their relationship as it was, but she clearly wasn't ready to think of anything more stable.

She was still hurting over her brother's death…and perhaps there was something more. He rather thought she might have been on the rebound from an unhappy love affair when she'd gone to stay with her sister in South Africa, which meant that he was just going to have to be patient.

A wry smile curved his mouth as he walked into the hospital. He'd been so sure he hadn't wanted a serious relationship, so careful not to get involved, and now…he was well and truly caught.

'Hello, Dr Grant,' a voice said just behind him, making him start out of his reverie. 'Are you coming to the dance on Saturday?'

He turned to find himself gazing into the openly admiring eyes of Staff Nurse Browne.

'Yes, as a matter of fact, Sister Hastings and I are attending together,' he said, smiling inwardly as he saw her eyes widen. He knew that it would be all over the hospital by that evening, and he found the idea very amusing. 'Yes, I'm actually looking forward to it this year. Excuse me, Anne, I must get on. I have to get back for surgery after I've visited my patient.'

It was Friday morning. Philip had dashed into Cambridge to buy the presents he'd missed last time— and to get something for Megan. He hadn't bought her anything on his last trip because he hadn't really expected to be in her company over Christmas, but things had changed since then.

His gift to Megan was suddenly uppermost in his mind. It had to be special, and it had to be right. No fancy black underwear. Seeing her in the kind of thing that sprang to mind, that would be a gift to himself, not her. He wanted to get something she would really appreciate—not perfume, because she always wore the same one. Not a handbag or gloves or a sweater. He had bought a beautiful cashmere for Susan, and didn't want to repeat himself. That would look as if he hadn't given Megan's present a lot of thought. Perhaps a piece of jewellery…

He stopped outside the next jeweller's shop he came to and stood gazing into the window for several minutes, dazzled by the bright lights and the festive glitter. A tray of diamond rings took his eye, and he frowned over his thoughts. What did he buy for a woman he admired? A woman who didn't want a serious relationship… At this stage, he wouldn't admit, even to himself, that it was anything more.

'What are you looking at?' Susan's voice startled him, making him look round. 'Philip! Engagement rings already? I didn't think you were such a fast worker. May I offer my congratulations?'

Philip glared at his sister. 'No, you may not, Susan. I *am* looking for a Christmas present for Megan. I'm thinking of jewellery, but not a ring. So you can just put that idea right out of your mind. Megan is a colleague and a friend—nothing more.'

'Pull the other one, it has bells on it,' Susan said dryly. 'I've seen the way you two look at each other. You may not be looking for a ring just yet—but you will.'

'Go away, Susan. And, please, stop being a match-maker.'

'I'm going,' she said. 'And I don't need to be a match-maker—you're doing very well all by yourself.'

And with that she sailed off, clearly feeling she had scored a hit.

Philip laughed ruefully as he went inside the jeweller's shop. He was very fond of his sister, but she did want to know a little too much at times.

'Yes, sir?' the sales assistant said as she came up to him. 'May I help you?'

'Yes, please,' Philip replied. 'I want a present for a lady. Something good, but not a ring. I thought perhaps a gold bracelet. Can you show me your better range, please?'

'Yes, sir. Do you prefer a solid bangle or a link effect?'

'I was looking at the bangles in the window,' Philip replied, 'but I would really like to see several different types so that I can choose.'

'Of course, sir. I'll show you our selection of bangles first. Just one moment, please…'

Philip watched as she went off to fetch a tray. After he'd chosen Megan's present, he must get something for Mike. That would be easy. Anything wearable would probably be acceptable, from the look of his brother-in-law's wardrobe!

CHAPTER SIX

PHILIP glanced in the mirror as he finished dressing that Saturday evening. He was wearing a plain, dark evening suit which he had worn before, but he had bought himself a new shirt.

He turned from the mirror and went downstairs, picking up his pager and slipping it into his jacket pocket out of habit. He was officially off duty that evening, but you never knew for sure if you might be called out.

One of the nurses at the practice had come up with a good idea at the last staff meeting. She'd suggested that part-time locums might be taken on by the practice to provide cover for the doctors at night. It was an idea that was catching on at other surgeries, but had never been considered by Philip or his partners before. It would be an added expense, of course, but the partnership was doing well and he believed they could afford to take the step which would guarantee each partner some free time.

It wasn't something that had bothered Philip before, but he rather thought it might in the future. He was smiling as he went out to his car and drove the short distance to the village.

Megan looked fantastic. There was simply no other word that would adequately describe her that evening. Philip could hardly keep his hands off her. Just looking at her made him go weak inside. She really was a very lovely, desirable woman.

'I'm not much good at describing clothes,' Philip told her with a mischievous grin, 'but if Susan asks me what you were wearing, I would have to say that dress was slinky. Very sexy!'

Megan glanced down at herself. Her dress was black, a soft jersey that clung to her body in a flattering way and was supported by a swathe of silk over one shoulder, leaving the other bare.

'Is it too much for the hospital dance?' Megan asked anxiously. 'I bought it ages ago but never wore it. I could change into a long skirt and blouse if you prefer?'

'Don't you dare!' Philip said. 'I wasn't complaining, believe me. That dress looks wonderful on you. I'm going to be the envy of every man in the place tonight.'

Megan smiled but shook her head. 'I very much doubt that,' she said. 'There are a lot of pretty girls at the hospital, Phil. You just haven't bothered to look.'

He laughed but didn't answer. Pretty was one thing. Megan had something more. She was both beautiful and sensual, the kind of woman any man would want. If she didn't know that, the man in her past must have been an odd sort of lover.

As they drove to the hotel where the dinner dance was being held, they talked shop. One of Philip's patients had come into the hospital late that afternoon with a Colles' fracture.

'She said you told her you suspected a wrist fracture,' Megan told him. 'She's had manipulation and was taken to the plaster room just as I was leaving. She stopped me and introduced herself, asked me to tell you you were right.'

'Miss Wright asked you to pass on the message?' Philip chuckled. 'She's the games mistress at a junior school, you know, and was injured showing her girls how to turn handsprings. She thought it was just a sprain. I persuaded her to take the time to have an X-ray—but why tell you? Rather odd, isn't it? It's not as if you're attached to the X-ray department.'

'She said she knew we were friends.'

'We've been seen together,' Philip said. He shot an amused glance at her. 'It's a small community. They are starting to gossip—do you mind?'

Megan smiled and shook her head 'Not unless you do?'

'I rather like it,' Philip said. 'It will do my street cred a lot of good to be seen with a beautiful woman. Stop me sinking into middle age and obscurity.'

Megan gurgled with laughter. 'I don't think you're in any danger of that just yet, Phil.'

He smiled but made no reply, drawing his car into an available parking space at the rear of the large, prestigious hotel where the event was being held. The hotel was one of the best in the district and set in attractive grounds that bordered the river. There were lights in the shrubbery, and at one point it was possible to walk along a path and, in the summer, watch the punts being lazily propelled by students and tourists.

Megan took his arm as they walked into the reception area. She smiled at a young girl who came to take her wrap, looking happy and relaxed. Philip thought it was the first time he'd seen her without a faint trace of sadness in her eyes, and that made him feel good. Perhaps she was beginning to forget the things that had hurt her, and if he was helping her to do that he was glad.

The tables for dinner were set with red and gold Christmas decorations, and there was a small gift of chocolates beside the plate for each lady. Soft music was playing, but as yet no one had taken their seat. There was a feeling of excitement in the air, and people were standing in little groups, talking shop, sipping their drinks and generally enjoying the evening.

However, as Megan and Philip walked in, there was a loud roll of drums and the Master of Ceremonies formally requested everyone to be seated.

Philip had reserved his usual table in the corner. He apologised to Megan as they threaded their way through the crowd.

'I should have asked for a better table,' he said with a rueful twist of his lips. 'You deserve to see and be seen.'

'This suits me fine.' Megan looked at him, her eyes bright with laughter. 'I think we can claim to have been well and truly noticed. I knew you were considered the most elusive of the hospital bachelors, Phil, but I didn't realise our presence here this evening would cause quite so much interest.'

'Elusive?' He arched his brows, very amused. 'Really? That makes me feel rather exciting and mysterious. Tell me, what else do they say?'

Megan shook her head, mischief in her eyes. 'It wouldn't be good for you, Phil.'

The waiter came to take their order just then, and the subject was dropped. The menu was rather predictable— smoked salmon, followed by roast turkey with all the trimmings, or a vegetarian alternative.

'I'm going for tradition,' Philip said. 'I expect I shall be eating it several times this coming week, but that's no hardship as far as I'm concerned.'

'I like turkey,' Megan said, 'but I think I'll try the vegetarian roast this time.'

'White or red wine? There's a rather fine white Bordeaux on the list here.'

'Sounds lovely.'

One or two couples were already dancing. 'Shall we?' Philip asked as the waiter left with their order. 'Or would you prefer to wait until later?'

'No time like the present…'

Philip smiled as he led her onto the central area which had been cleared for dancing. He was conscious that many heads had turned in their direction, but as he put his arm about Megan's waist everything else faded into the background.

Her perfume wafted towards him like the scent of flowers on a summer's breeze, tantalising and delicious. She felt so good in his arms, so light and soft as she danced. He had never particularly enjoyed dancing in the past, but he wanted this new, glorious sensation to go on for ever.

They were both smiling as they went back to their table. Philip tasted the wine, nodding absently to the hovering waiter. He had no idea what he was tasting— anything would have been like nectar at that moment.

It was the happiest he had felt for a long, long time. He glanced across the table at Megan, and she smiled. She looked as if she was enjoying herself, too.

They danced between courses, taking the floor twice during the meal. More and more couples were getting up now, the atmosphere mellowing as wine flowed and the evening wore on.

'May I steal Megan away from you for this dance?'

Philip had been sipping his coffee and hadn't noticed Robert Crawley approaching their table. Earlier, everyone had stuck to their own partners, but now they were beginning to mix, to move about the room, to talk with friends.

Philip felt slight annoyance at the way the request had

been put to him, rather than to Megan herself, but did his best to hide it.

'Of course—if Megan would like to dance?' He looked across the table at her, his brows lifted.

'Thank you, Robert,' Megan said, smiling up at him. 'You don't mind, Phil? I did want a word with Robert…'

'Please, do.' Philip smiled easily and waved her away.

He did mind, of course. He minded like hell, but he wasn't going to let it show. Jealousy was an ugly thing. Especially as he knew he had no reason—or right—to feel it.

'Hi. Been deserted?'

Philip glanced up as he heard the voice. Anne Browne was wearing a short, skimpy silver dress that left very little to the imagination. He had seen her dancing earlier with a young man he didn't know but believed was a physiotherapist at the hospital.

'Just for the moment,' he replied, trying to hide his chagrin. 'Not dancing yourself, Anne?'

'If you're asking, yes, please,' she said cheekily.

Philip hadn't intended to ask, but his casual inquiry could have been taken as an invitation and left him with little choice. He couldn't refuse without being unnecessarily rude.

'Why not?' he said, and stood up.

His dance with the young staff nurse was uncomfortable for Philip to say the least. She draped herself all over him, and he felt an acute desire to escape from her clinging arms and the strong, musky smell of her perfume. Fortunately, the dance ended in a very short time, having been halfway through before they stood up, and he was able to thank her and return to his table.

Megan glanced up as he sat down, her eyebrows lifting.

'I feel as if I've been eaten alive,' he murmured softly. 'Never again!'

'What did you expect?' Megan asked, a disapproving note in her voice. 'The poor girl is crazy about you. Has been for ages. Everyone knows that.'

'Do they?' Philip frowned. He felt he was being reprimanded and wasn't sure why. Surely not just for dancing with the girl? 'I'm sorry. I had no idea.'

'No, of course not,' Megan said. She seemed angry. 'Men—particularly powerful, attractive men like you—never seem to realise what others feel. You smile at Anne and ask her how she is one day, appearing to show interest, then ignore her the next. That's cruel, Phil. Why ask her to dance if you didn't want to?'

To say that he hadn't really asked wasn't much of an excuse. Philip had been aware of Anne's interest—he just hadn't taken her seriously, believing that she was the same with most men. The idea that the young staff nurse might be breaking her heart over him was both shocking and disturbing.

'Put like that, it sounds as if I've been thoughtless,' Philip said. 'Believe me, I never meant to hurt her. I happen to like the girl. I'm just not attracted to her in a physical way.'

'I know you didn't mean to hurt her,' Megan said, 'but you did it just the same.'

Philip saw that the shadows were back in her eyes. She wasn't just angry about his careless remarks concerning Anne Browne—this went much deeper.

'I'm sorry I've made you angry, Megan.'

She met his gaze for a moment, then flushed. 'No, it wasn't you, Phil, not really. It was just a memory.'

'Do you want to talk about it? Shall we leave?'

'No.' She lifted her head, a glint of pride in her eyes.

'Forgive me. I spoke out of turn just now. Shall we dance? It would be a pity to spoil such a lovely evening.'

'It hasn't been spoiled,' Philip said, standing up and offering her his hand. 'I've enjoyed myself, Megan. We'll agree not to argue and we'll forget it, shall we?'

'Yes, of course. It was silly really.'

He made no reply, showing that he considered the subject closed. He wasn't going to let the small incident ruin their evening if he could help it.

It had changed things, though. Philip was still aware of how much he wanted Megan, how much she was beginning to mean to him, but he was also very conscious of the shadows in her past.

Just what had happened to make her carry this ache inside her? Had it been the tragic illness and death of her brother, or was there more to it?

Philip was thoughtful as he parked outside Megan's cottage in the early hours of Sunday morning.

'You are coming in?' she asked, as he sat for a moment without moving.

'Are you sure you want me to?' His expression was serious as he looked at her, searching her face. 'It's what I want, Megan. I want to stay—very much. But you don't have to—'

She leaned towards him, brushing her lips over his. 'Don't be a growly bear, Phil. Forget what I said earlier. I'm not a child. I know exactly what I'm doing. Please, stay. I want you to.'

'Then I'm staying,' he murmured throatily. He drew back and looked at her, a wicked gleam in his eyes. 'Only...do you think we could possibly make it as far as the bedroom this time? I had a crick in the neck for hours after sleeping on that sofa.'

'Oh, yes,' Megan said, her voice husky, her eyes smoky with desire. 'I'm sure we can if we're quick. Come on, Phil, we're wasting time. Don't forget, you're playing Father Christmas this afternoon...'

Philip laughed. 'That sounds promising,' he said. 'I can't remember the last time I stayed in bed for the whole of Sunday morning.'

'Then it's time you did.' Her eyes were wicked, challenging him.

Megan got out of the car, waiting on the path while Philip locked the door and joined her. She smiled and held out her hand to him, their fingers interlocking as he took it.

'No dramas tonight,' she whispered huskily. 'Just a nice time for us both.'

They had made it to the bed this time, and it had been very nice. More than nice, Philip thought, aware of Megan sleeping beside him. He could still taste her, still feel the imprint of her breasts, the warmth of her flesh pressed against him. In fact, he knew that for him the act of sex had never been so satisfying, so fulfilling.

Megan was a very beautiful, loving woman. She gave so much, so unstintingly.

Philip listened to her steady breathing. She hadn't wept this time. She'd nestled into his arms, whispering that it had been good for her and that he'd made her happy, then had fallen asleep.

He envied her her ability to sleep so suddenly. She was like a little cat, golden and soft, curled up in the safety of his arms, and that was where he wanted her. He was aware of a need to protect her, to keep her from harm.

He closed his eyes, drifting towards sleep himself.

Then he felt Megan jerk. A moan escaped her and he realised she was dreaming. She cried out as if in pain and he tensed as he heard her cry something aloud.

'No, please, don't,' she muttered. 'Don't leave me…don't do this to me…'

A choking sound issued from her lips as though she were crying. Philip put his arms around her, gathering her closer. She seemed to half wake, then burrowed into him, her face pressed into his shoulder.

'It's all right, my little love,' he whispered against her hair. 'You're not alone. I'm with you. I've got you safe. No one is going to hurt you while I'm here.'

Megan gave no sign of having heard him, but she settled. There was no more jerking, no more moaning. He stroked her hair until he was quite sure she was sleeping, then let himself drift away again.

Megan had been badly hurt by someone. Philip was more or less certain of it now. Grief was a part of that hurt, but not the whole. He'd sensed that she was hiding something, and now he knew a man had been responsible for the barrier she used to shut him out at times.

Somehow that made him more determined. He would find a way of breaking that barrier down. He would win Megan's trust, teach her to rely on him, believe in him, to know he wasn't going to hurt her—maybe even to care. He had to, because he cared for her. More than he had thought possible.

Philip found bacon, mushrooms and tomatoes in Megan's fridge. He cooked breakfast while she was in the shower, presenting it with a flourish as she walked in, still drying her hair on a towel.

'I usually just have some toast,' she said, amused by

his industry. 'Still, I suppose it's a bit late for breakfast—this is more of a brunch.'

'Definitely brunch,' Philip replied. 'If you will stay in
bed half the morning…'

'And who kept me there?' she demanded, but her eyes
were full of laughter. 'Perhaps we both deserve something substantial after such strenuous exercise.'

'The best, according to the experts,' he quipped. 'I
certainly feel A1 this morning.'

'Up to your ordeal this afternoon?'

'As much as I'll ever be.' Philip pulled a wry face.
'Why did I let Jennifer talk me into it? I must have been
mad.'

'You fraud!' Megan accused in a teasing voice.
'You're looking forward to it. You love kids and giving
presents. You were born for the job—it's your vocation
in life.'

'Why didn't I think of that before?' Philip asked,
looking struck by the idea. 'I would only need to work
for a few weeks in the year. I could spend the rest of
my time having a lie-in in the mornings.'

'And die of boredom in a couple of months,' Megan
mocked. 'You need to work, Phil. It's your life, your
reason for being. Everyone knows that you're dedicated
to the job.'

'Do they indeed?' He arched his brows at her. 'You
shouldn't believe all you hear on the hospital grapevine,
my love. I am dedicated to my work, as much as most
doctors, but I enjoy other things—good music, dining
out… And I'm as bad as any other man when there's
an England football match on the telly.'

'I shall take that as a warning to stay clear of your
house whenever the World Cup is on,' Megan said,

pouring coffee into two mugs. 'I am definitely not a football fan.'

'You haven't been to my cottage yet,' Philip said, looking at her thoughtfully. 'I'll cook dinner for you one night.' He hesitated, not quite sure of where they went next. 'What shall we do for the rest of the day? I'll have to go home and change at some point...'

'Go when you've eaten,' Megan said. 'I've got some chores I have to do, Phil, but I'll come to the party with you. As moral support, if nothing else.'

She was smiling as she dismissed him. Philip took it with good grace. They were getting on, getting to know each other gradually. At least on this occasion they had spent time talking as well as making love. That was progress. He mustn't be greedy, he mustn't push too hard. She needed space to sort herself out, time to let old wounds heal.

'Good thinking,' he said. 'I've got a few things to do myself, Megan. Shall I give you a hand with the washing-up before I leave?'

'I have a dishwasher,' she said. 'It came with the house. I shall just throw everything in and let the machine do the work.'

'Then I'll leave you to it...'

He kissed her goodbye a few minutes later, a little reluctant but knowing she was right. He did have things to do, and so did she. They hadn't yet reached the stage where they could do them together.

Philip was thoughtful as he drove home. Would they ever get to the stage where they might consider moving in together?

He quite liked the idea of them living in the same house, of waking up every morning to find Megan beside him. It would be nice not to be alone every night. They would both go on working, of course. Megan was a career woman—or was she?

He seemed to know so many things about her instinctively, but in other ways she was still like a closed book.

The children's party was a riot, the kids screaming, being sick, jumping all over everything and generally creating havoc—a sure sign that it was a success.

Philip performed his duties perfectly. He arrived on cue, humping his sack into the midst of the youngsters, and handed out the presents, which had fortunately been labelled in clear writing.

'You're not Father Christmas,' one little boy said, pulling at his beard. 'You're Dr Philip.'

'I'm very sorry,' Philip said. 'Father Christmas had an accident. He asked me to stand in for him, but he has promised to be well in time for Christmas Eve.'

'Did you make him better?' The boy's eyes were wide and curious. 'Did he fall down the chimney?'

'Well, I did my best to make him better,' Philip replied. 'I think it was the stairs he fell down, actually. But I'm sure your presents will arrive on Christmas Day.'

The boy nodded and ran off, clutching his parcel. His mother looked at Philip and shook her head, seeming to apologise for the inquisition.

'So, how did it feel?' Megan asked as they left after the present-giving. 'Are you still thinking of applying for the job on a permanent basis?'

'A professional Father Christmas would have his own beard,' Philip said as he drove them to Susan's house for supper afterwards. 'I shall have to consider the idea next year.'

'You haven't let them rope you in?' Megan mocked. 'Sucker for punishment, aren't you?'

'Didn't you hear them say I was the best ever? How could I refuse?'

She smiled, giving him a pensive look. 'I'm never quite sure when you're joking, Phil. Those kids were perfect monsters, but I must admit you were good with them. You love children, don't you?'

'Yes, I suppose I always have. Don't you?' He shot her a curious look. 'I got the idea that you were fond of Beth's children.'

'Yes, I am,' Megan admitted. She turned her face away as if to hide her thoughts. 'But I doubt if I shall ever have any of my own.'

'It's not too late yet.'

'No, perhaps not.'

The tone of her voice warned Philip not to push things. Besides, they'd arrived at his sister's home. Susan already had the door open and the children were rushing out to greet them.

'Come in, come in,' Susan cried, welcoming them both with a smile. 'You must be exhausted after all that, Phil. Jodie wanted to come when she heard about you being Father Christmas, but we're not actually members of the club. I told her she couldn't. She would have told everyone you were her uncle.'

'I was rumbled by one astute lad anyway,' Philip said, and kissed her. 'It seems the real Father Christmas has a proper beard.'

'Planning to grow one for next year? I dare say they'll rope you in again.' She looked at Megan as she ushered them into the sitting room. 'You will be here for Christmas Day, won't you?'

'Yes. I'm looking forward to it.'

'Sit down and I'll— Oh, damn!'

Her oath was caused by Philip's pager, which had started to go off.

'Excuse me,' he said. 'May I use your phone, Susan? My mobile's in the car.'

'Of course.' Susan pulled a face at Megan as he passed her. 'This is always happening. Just when you think we're going to have a nice evening together. Still, that's what you get for having a doctor for a brother.'

Philip made a quick call, then went back into the sitting room where the others were talking.

'I have to go,' he said. 'A child with head injuries. I'm sorry, Megan. Stay and have your supper. I know Susan will run you home later.'

'Are you sure I can't be of help to you?' She half rose, as if prepared to go with him.

'No, I don't think so. I may be some hours. It sounds serious. You won't want to be kept hanging around all night. I know the family well. I shall probably go to the hospital with them if it's as bad as it sounds. They'll need moral support.'

'You get off,' Susan said. 'Don't worry about Megan. We can look after her.'

Philip nodded. He looked at Megan apologetically.

'Sorry about this,' he said, 'but it was my turn to be on call this evening. I'll phone you as soon as I can.'

'Please, just go,' Megan said. 'I understand, Phil. Naturally, your work must come first.'

Philip nodded but didn't say anything. He couldn't kiss her or say much more than he already had, without seeming to make too much of it. He wasn't sure she would want him to, not in front of Susan and the family.

As he went out to the car and started the engine, he wondered how Megan really felt about being abandoned at his sister's house. Helen would have hated it, of course. There would have been a row later. But Megan was a professional nurse. Unlike his ex-wife, she would understand.

His thoughts turned to his patient. Head injuries were one of the most common forms of injury in infants and children. The flexible structure of a child's skull usually protected the brain from permanent damage, but in some cases it could be more serious. Often slight injuries weren't reported, which could lead to acquired disability.

In this particular case the mother was frantic. Her son was a very active child who had already spent a night in hospital after a similar injury some months back. Philip knew a part of her fear was that she or her partner might be accused of inflicting the wound. He also knew that she would never harm her child, and he didn't believe the child's father was violent either, but he would need to be sure of the facts.

If he was satisfied in his own mind that there hadn't been abuse, he would make sure his report was accepted at the hospital. These days parents could often have a terrible time because someone suspected them of abusing their child without good reason.

It was a difficult field for social workers and medical personnel alike. Neglect a potentially dangerous situation and a child could die—bring false accusations unnecessarily and it could ruin the lives of the whole family.

He accelerated slightly. For the moment his personal problems were put to one side. His patient's needs were paramount. He would think about Megan later.

Philip's thoughts returned to Megan when he returned home late that evening. He had stayed at the hospital until the results of the first scans had come through. There was no evidence of shaken baby syndrome, the nasty bang on the forehead likely to have occurred as a result of the child climbing up onto a chair and tipping it over, as his mother had claimed.

It looked as though the boy had escaped any lasting damage, but they were keeping him in for observation for a couple of days just to be sure. And that was where the new children's unit at the Chestnuts would have been so useful, Philip thought. It would have saved the mother having to travel all the way to Cambridge, though she was staying put for the night anyway.

Philip had left her there after making sure everything was under control. He hadn't received any more calls on his pager while he was at Addenbrookes, but on his way back to the village another urgent message reached him. This time it was from Mrs Bettaway's daughter. She thought her mother had had another stroke and was very upset.

When Philip reached the house he took one look at Mrs Bettaway and knew it was already too late. He made a brief examination and issued a death certificate, doing his best to comfort her daughter who was naturally in tears.

'At least she was with you,' he said. 'You brought her here. She didn't have to die in a nursing home. That's the very best you could do for her, my dear. We always knew she might have another stroke soon, and that it might be fatal. You made her last days good ones. You should take comfort from that.'

'Thank you, Doctor.' Eileen blew her nose hard. 'She had a good life, we know that—but I shall miss her.'

'I should think the whole village will miss her,' Philip

said. 'Are you all right? Do you need any help with the arrangements?'

'No, we can manage,' she said, 'but thank you for asking. My mother was fond of you, Dr Grant. She always said we were lucky to have you, that a man like you could have been in private practice or in a top job as a consultant.'

'Never appealed to me,' he replied with a smile. 'I must leave you now, but don't hesitate to ring me if there's anything further I can do.'

She smiled and he went out into a frosty night, driving home with care because the roads were slippery again. He was feeling tired and a little sad as he went into the house. So many of his patients were friends and he hated losing them…

He glanced at his watch. It was nearly midnight, too late to phone Megan now. She would probably be sleeping, and she was on early shift the next morning. He didn't want to wake her, even though he desperately wanted to talk to her.

As he undressed and slipped into bed, Philip was aware of a fierce ache inside him. He wanted Megan to be there in his bed, wanted to feel the warmth of her there beside him, to hold her in his arms.

He hadn't expected to feel this way about her. He'd imagined it would be easy to keep their relationship on a casual footing, but it was much harder than he'd expected.

Yet he knew that he had to be careful. Megan was still vulnerable, still hurting, and he would never forgive himself if he did something to make her pain harder to bear…

CHAPTER SEVEN

PHILIP finished surgery on Monday evening. He needed to buy a couple of small items from the shop and drove into the village, before going home. As he passed Megan's house he saw Robert Crawley's car parked in the drive behind hers.

He frowned, wondering why the farmer was visiting at this hour. Megan had seemed eager to dance with him the other evening, had wanted to talk to him about something—was she reconsidering her decision not to encourage his attentions?

Surely not? She wouldn't have asked Philip to stay after the dance if she'd wanted to finish their affair. He was disgusted with himself for even thinking such a thing, but couldn't help his feelings of jealousy. The trouble was, he didn't really know where he stood with Megan.

In Philip's book they were having an affair, something that could turn into a much deeper relationship, given time, but he couldn't be certain that Megan felt the same way. It had all happened so fast that Philip was still in a bit of a spin, still trying to catch his breath.

It would be much easier if he could open his heart to her, tell her how he felt and ask her what her plans were for the future—but he was afraid of pushing her too far too fast.

He swallowed his chagrin that she appeared to be entertaining Robert Crawley and drove home. He wasn't on call that evening, and he thought he might pop up to

131

the Chestnuts and spend some time with Matthew. With any luck, his friend might be able to leave hospital for Christmas.

The last few days before Christmas were exceptionally busy for Philip. It seemed that all his patients wanted appointments before the holiday, as if to make sure every little ache and pain was checked out so that nothing could disrupt the festivities. Coughs, colds and stomach bugs made up two thirds of his list, but most of his patients brought greetings cards and seemed to have come as much to wish him a happy Christmas as to seek treatment.

In the old days grateful patients often gave presents of eggs or vegetables from their gardens to their doctor. For days now Philip had returned to find small gifts on his doorstep, things like bunches of holly and mistletoe, a box of apples or a sack of carrots with the earth still clinging to them. All were left anonymously, but Philip had a good idea where they had come from.

He was deeply touched by the gifts, not because he needed or wanted them—most edible items found their way to Susan's kitchen—but because it showed that he was a part of the community, that his patients appreciated the time he gave them.

His social commitments always increased at this time of year. He dined with both his partners on separate occasions that week, and on another occasion took his sister to a smart cocktail party Mike was unable to attend. He also attended Peter's school carol service and helped Susan to fetch her Christmas tree from the garden centre.

Despite all the frenetic activity, Philip managed to phone Megan several times. On three occasions her answerphone was switched on for the whole evening. He left messages, but when she eventually rang back he had been called out to a patient. Finally, he managed to catch her at the hospital on the morning of Christmas Eve.

'Oh…' She was surprised to see him. 'You don't usually visit in the mornings.'

'No, not as a rule, but things are hectic this week. I'm taking surgery this afternoon, and I'm on call this evening. I just wanted to confirm the arrangements for tomorrow—I'll pick you up about twelve, shall I?'

'Yes, that's just right,' Megan said. 'It will give me time to make a few telephone calls and deliver a couple of presents myself.'

Philip nodded. Was he imagining things, or did she seem to have retreated behind that barrier again?

'I'm sorry I didn't manage to talk to you earlier in the week,' he said. 'It's been a busy week, and somehow I couldn't seem to catch you at home.'

'Yes, it has been busy,' Megan agreed. 'I've been seeing a few old friends. There are always demands on one's time at Christmas. I've been out for drinks and a couple of meals this week. I did try to return your calls, but you were out, too.'

'Yes, I know. It must have been fate.'

Philip wondered whether Megan's friends were female, then dismissed the doubts as unworthy. He had no reason to be jealous of her friendship with Robert Crawley or anyone else for that matter, no right to expect to monopolise her time.

'Well, I mustn't delay you,' he said as she glanced at her watch. 'I'll see you tomorrow.'

'Doctors' rounds,' Megan said, picking up a clipboard. 'Sorry to rush away, Phil. I'm looking forward to tomorrow.'

'Yes, so am I.'

Philip was thoughtful as he drove back to the village. Was Megan's apparent reserve because she was angry at being abandoned at Susan's the other evening? He'd noticed she'd looked tired, as if she hadn't slept well recently. Her eyes had been shadowed and he wondered if she'd been overworking or perhaps didn't feel quite right—but surely she would have said something if she'd been unwell? Malaria was a nasty illness, and if she was getting even mild attacks, it must drag her down. Or was there another reason for her withdrawal?

Was she beginning to regret their affair? Philip had an uncomfortable feeling that something was wrong, but he couldn't think what he had done to upset her—unless it was because he'd had to leave her at his sister's house.

Somehow that didn't make sense. Megan was a professional nurse. She understood that patients came first in an emergency. So what had gone wrong?

Philip lay for a while without sleeping, thinking about Matthew and about Megan. They had both suffered personal traumas, and both needed time to sort themselves out.

He'd asked Matthew to come and stay over Christmas, when it had been decided that he was going to be allowed home for the festive holiday, but Matthew had surprised him by announcing he was going to stay with a friend.

'A woman friend,' Matthew had said, grinning. 'Megan rang Fanny and told her I needed looking after, and she invited me to stay with her for as long as I like.'

'Just remember you've been very ill,' Philip had warned. 'And don't do anything I wouldn't...'

'Which gives me loads of scope,' Matthew had said with a grin. 'When am I going to wish you happy, Phil?'

'That remains to be seen.'

He'd smiled mysteriously at his friend's curiosity, but Philip was beginning to be aware of a need within himself, a need he was finding very difficult to suppress.

He needed a sign that Megan was serious about their affair. In the beginning, all he'd wanted to do had been to comfort her. Making love had seemed like a good idea, and he hadn't believed it would commit either of them, but now Philip was beginning to want more. Much more than a casual affair.

It wasn't fair of him, he knew that. Megan wasn't ready for a serious relationship, she'd made that clear from the start. Philip had to be patient, he knew that it was fair and right that he should be…but perhaps he might try to take things a few steps further.

A groan escaped him. He *was* being unfair. He'd promised himself he wouldn't rush things, wouldn't put pressure on her, and he had to stick to that, otherwise he might lose her.

Philip tried to block out his thoughts, but they would keep tormenting him. Megan wasn't in love with him, he knew that. She'd turned to him for comfort, a shoulder to cry on—except that she seldom cried. She was a strong woman, fiercely independent and able to stand on her own two feet. She just needed a friend, someone to rely on, to help her through a bad time. A man she could feel comfortable with, a man she could trust.

Philip pulled a wry face in the darkness.

He wanted Megan here, he wanted her in his arms, to hear her saying the words he needed her to say…

He was a damned fool! He'd never been this way over Helen, hadn't thought it was possible that he could suffer such agonies of uncertainty. He'd always been in absolute control of his life, sure of where he was going and what he wanted. Good grief, he was like a teenager, mooning over some film star!

Philip's sense of humour came to his rescue. If he didn't get some sleep, it would soon be morning!

Megan was wearing a pair of tight-fitting white trousers, a long, matching fluffy jumper, a wide red leather belt cinched round her waist and red leather ankle boots.

'You look wonderful,' Philip said when she opened the door to him. 'Very Christmassy.'

'Thank you,' she replied, smiling at him. Her eyes were free of shadows and he wondered if he'd mistaken her mood the previous day. She seemed pleased to see him that morning. 'You look rather smart yourself, Phil.'

'It's the jacket,' Philip said. 'My old suede jacket has become rather shabby, and I decided I had better get a new one. So this is my Christmas present to myself.'

'Well, I like it very much,' she said, stroking the soft brown suede approvingly. Her perfume wafted towards him enticingly. 'I have a gift for you, Phil—shall I give it to you now? Or do we keep them for later?'

'I've got a couple of carriers of presents in the car,' Philip replied. 'We usually exchange them when I get there. The children open a few first thing, of course, but the grown-ups wait until we're all together. Unless you'd rather have yours now?'

'Let's wait for the others,' Megan said, her eyes bright with laughter. 'It will be more fun that way. I bought things for Susan and the children, and Mike, too.'

'The kids are going to be thoroughly spoiled this year.'

Megan laughed. She grabbed a red wool jacket, and Philip picked up the carrier bag she indicated, taking it out to the car for her. The church bells were ringing, and people were hurrying by on foot and in their cars. Philip waved to various people he knew, and someone hooted as they went past.

When they got to Susan's house they saw the Christmas tree in the window—it was bright with glass balls, with a fairy on top and strands of twinkling lights.

'Mike managed to get the lights going this year,' Philip remarked with a wry laugh. 'Or perhaps he had help. Susan was threatening to buy a new set.'

The children descended on them with whoops of joy, dragging Megan into the sitting room to look at the toys they'd already received that morning, while Philip brought the carrier bags into the hall.

'Come and have a drink of egg-nog,' Susan said as she saw her brother struggling. 'Shall I put these under the tree as usual?'

'That bag belongs to Megan,' Philip said. 'Better ask her what she wants to do with that first, though I expect she'll want to go along with the rest of us...'

He joined the others in the sitting room. Mike was stretched out on the floor, playing with a radio-controlled car which was supposed to be Peter's, and Megan was examining Jodie's new pram with interest.

Philip smiled and went over to sit beside Megan on the sofa. Susan carried in a tray of drinks, setting them on the coffee-table.

'Everyone helps themselves,' she said. 'Dinner won't be for another hour or so yet, so we've plenty of time to get slightly boozy. Even you, Phil. You aren't on call today so no excuses.'

'I still have to drive,' Philip said, 'but I'll have some wine with dinner. No egg-nog for me, but you must try it, Megan. It's very good, providing you have a strong head. This is none of your shop-bought stuff. Susan makes it herself—so be warned.'

'It's delicious,' Megan said, sipping hers carefully. 'Much better than you can buy.'

'Can we have our presents now?'

Jodie's demand brought a laugh from her mother. She looked at Megan, her smile indulgent and slightly mocking.

'Shall we get it over? We'll get no peace until they've torn the very last scrap of paper off their parcels.'

'I'm looking forward to it,' Megan replied with a smile. 'I miss seeing my sister's children this Christmas. We had a lot of fun last year when I was with them.'

'You must miss them terribly,' Susan said, nodding agreement. 'Christmas just isn't the same without children. But never mind—perhaps you'll have some of your own before too long.' She directed an arch look towards Philip.

Megan's cheeks were slightly pink, but she didn't say anything. She didn't have to because Mike had given the children permission to hand out the parcels, and Jodie had brought her a small pile, pushing them onto her lap.

'Are these all for me?' she asked, looking surprised.

'There's one from Uncle Philip, one from Mum and Dad, and one from me and Peter,' Jodie chanted. 'That's three. I've got lots and lots more than you.'

'That's good,' Megan said. 'Let's see you open some of them.'

'You've got to open this one first,' Jodie insisted, pressing Philip's parcel into her hands. 'Then I can open one next. We all have to open one in turn.'

Megan smiled, and untied the silver ribbon surrounding the beautifully wrapped parcel. She hesitated as she saw the jeweller's box inside, then opened it and gasped with pleasure.

'This is lovely, Phil,' she said, taking out the gold bangle and fastening it on her wrist. 'Gorgeous. I've always wanted a pretty bangle, but I've never had one before. Thank you so much…I shall always treasure it.'

'I'm glad you like it,' Philip said, smiling because she was obviously pleased. She hadn't said any of the usual things like, 'Oh, you shouldn't!' He took that as a good sign. 'Thank you for the shirt. It's just what I need to replace one that got torn recently…'

Megan laughed, her eyes meeting his in a shared joke. He knew she'd deliberately chosen a shirt like the one he'd been wearing the night he'd first stayed at her cottage, and he liked it that she'd wanted to remind him.

Susan was exclaiming over the cashmere sweater Philip had bought her. Mike had given her a silk scarf and some very expensive silk underwear, and when Megan opened her parcel from Susan and Mike she revealed that she, too, had been given a hand-printed silk scarf. Megan had bought Mike aftershave and an expensive perfume set for Susan.

'A Hermes scarf,' Susan was saying. 'I've always wanted one, Mike.' She reached over and kissed him.

The piles of torn paper had become scattered all over the floor. Megan helped Susan to pick them up while the men began a discussion about the various sports fixtures that were being held locally and would be shown on television the following day.

'May I help at all?' Megan asked, as Susan headed for the kitchen to check on the meal.

'No, stay there and play with the children,' Susan said. 'Everything is under control for the moment, and Mike will give me a hand with the dishing up later.'

'Look at my doll, Auntie Megan,' Jodie pleaded, tugging at her arm. 'Isn't she lovely? What shall I call her?'

'What would you like to call her?' Megan asked, settling down with the child on the floor. 'You did get a lot of lovely presents, didn't you, darling?'

'Lots and lots,' Jodie said. 'Look at this teddy Daddy gave me and the Beanies Uncle Philip bought, and…'

The list was endless. Philip turned his head to watch as the little girl claimed Megan's attention for the next half hour. She was so good with Jodie, really interested, and seemed to enjoy joining in the child's games.

'She's a born mother, your Megan,' Susan said approvingly as she came to sit on the arm of his chair. 'You're a lucky man, Phil. I hope you realise it…'

She'd spoken in a voice loud enough to carry. Philip knew that Megan must have heard, though she didn't give any sign of having done so. Mike was playing with Peter's cars, and he grinned at her, making some remark that made her laugh and look up.

Philip's heart jerked suddenly. She was so lovely, so natural. Especially when she forgot to remember the past, when she was happy and relaxed as now. Susan was right—she ought to be a mother. She deserved the chance to be happy.

Megan glanced across the room at him. He smiled and she nodded, then looked down again as Jodie said something to her.

Was he imagining it, or had there been something guarded about her eyes? He knew she must have heard Susan's comment about her being born to be a mother, and his sister had made several other pointed remarks which had made it clear that she believed they were a committed couple.

He wasn't sure how Megan felt about Susan's assumption that they would marry, and he hoped she didn't think that he'd given his sister reason to believe that such an outcome was imminent.

It was nearly nine o'clock that evening when they were at last allowed to leave. Philip stopped the car, then got out to open the door for Megan and follow her into her cottage.

'I thought we'd never get away,' he said. 'I'd hoped we might get to spend the afternoon together, Megan, but there was no question of leaving while the children were still up.'

'None at all,' Megan said, smiling at him. 'It was fun, Phil. I enjoyed it a lot. Thank you for taking me, and for giving me that wonderful bracelet.'

'It was nothing,' he said, his voice slightly husky. He wanted very much to kiss her at that moment, but hesitated because he sensed a withdrawal in her. 'I wanted something special—because you're a special person, Megan.'

'Thank you.' She turned away, heading towards the kitchen. 'I'll make some coffee, shall I? I think I need it after all Susan's egg-nog.'

'Yes, it can be lethal,' he replied. He glanced at the grate, where a fire had been laid. 'Shall I put a match to that for you?'

'Yes, please. The heating is on, but this place needs a fire to cheer it up. I'm not sure I shall stay here for another winter. I might buy somewhere—if I can find anything in my price range.'

Philip nodded, watching as she went through to the kitchen. Megan had been quiet since the children had gone off to bed, and he'd noticed her looking at him thoughtfully a couple of times…almost as if she could read his mind.

When she returned with two mugs of coffee, he was sitting by the fire, staring into the flames. Something had been on his mind for a while now, and he was wondering whether or not to bring it up.

'Phil…' Megan sounded hesitant as she picked up her coffee and began to sip it. 'I was wondering…would you mind very much if you didn't stay over tonight?'

Philip had been reaching for his mug, but he left it untouched, his eyes searching her face. 'Why—is something wrong?' he asked. He did mind, he minded very much, but he was very careful as he went on. 'We don't have to have sex if it's the wrong time or something— but I was hoping to be with you.'

'No, it isn't the wrong time of the month,' Megan said honestly. 'I just feel I need a break, Phil. What happened that night…it wasn't planned.'

'I know that, of course I do—but we're good together. I was hoping our relationship would develop, Megan. We seem to get on well and I'd hoped we—'

'Yes, we do, of course we do,' she said quickly. 'I've enjoyed being with you, Phil. It's nothing you've done, believe me.'

'Then why? Are you feeling unwell or something?'

'I do have a bit of a headache,' she said, her eyes avoiding his. 'It's nothing to worry about, but I— I'm sorry, Phil.' She stood up. 'I really would prefer to be alone tonight.'

Philip stood up. He was seized by an urge that would not be denied, even though he knew he should just give in gracefully and leave. He reached out for her, taking both her hands in his, holding them fast as he gazed into her face.

'I know it's too soon to say this,' he said, his throat tight with wanting her, 'but I'm afraid that if I don't the chance may pass and we'll just drift apart. I don't want that to happen, Megan. We haven't known each other long, but I've come to like and respect you—more than that, I care for you a great deal.'

'Please, Phil...' She flushed and tried to remove her hands, but he refused to let go. 'Not tonight.'

'I must say this,' he said. 'I'm not asking for an answer now, Megan. I'm willing to wait, for as long as it takes—but I want you to consider my proposition.'

'Proposition...' She glanced up at him, her eyes shadowed. 'I think I can guess, Phil.'

'I want you to be my partner or my wife, whichever you think you could live with,' Philip went on. 'I know Susan dropped some heavy hints today, and I'm sorry if she embarrassed you. I didn't give her any reason to think we might be considering moving in together because, to be honest, I hadn't really considered it myself until last night.' He took a deep breath. 'At first it was just meant to be a pleasant interlude—'

Megan smiled oddly. 'I know that, Phil. When I asked you to stay that night, I did so in the full knowledge that you had no intention of marrying anyone.'

'The hospital grapevine again!' He pulled a wry face. 'It may have been true for a while. I was wary of relationships after my divorce—but I've realised that life can be pretty empty if you don't learn to trust, Megan. I've been over Helen for a long time, but I couldn't be bothered with looking for someone else. Things have changed since I met you. I'm sick of being alone every night. I want a proper home, someone to share my life with—and children.' He touched her cheek. 'I know that's a lot to ask, but it's what I want—and I'd like you to be the one who shares the future with me.'

'I feel honoured.' Megan laughed as he pulled a face of disgust. 'No, don't look like that, Phil. I mean it. You're a terrific person, in your work and personally. I…like you a lot, and I trust you. That means more than you may think.'

'But?' He raised his brows, his heart wrenching with fear. 'Are you turning me down, Megan?'

'You said you were prepared to wait for your answer?'

'Yes, of course I am—as long as it takes.' He looked at her, suddenly eager. 'Does that mean you'll consider the idea?'

Megan was silent for a moment, then she nodded. 'I do need to think about this, Phil. I'm not making any promises…' She raised her head, meeting his eyes honestly. 'I expect you've heard the gossip about me?'

'I never listen,' he said, denying the few spiteful words he'd overheard. 'And I don't care. I know you've been hurt somehow. All I want is to make you happy.'

'I have been happy these past few days,' Megan said. 'Happier than I expected to be… But I still need time. If you're willing to give me that, I might be able to give you what you want.'

'Then I'll wait,' he said, and leaned towards her, gently kissing her lips. 'I think we could make a go of it, Megan. But I won't pressure you again. I promise.'

'I'll give you an answer as soon as I can,' she said, returning his kiss. 'It's been good, Phil. I've needed a friend, and you've certainly been that. Thank you.'

'*No,* thank you,' he said. 'I'll probably see you at the hospital tomorrow—but don't worry, I shan't expect you to give me an answer. I just want us to go on being close, the way we were.'

'We will,' she said softly. 'And perhaps there can be more.'

'I'll go now,' Philip said. He stroked her cheek softly. 'You're a beautiful woman, Megan. If someone hurt you, he was a fool.'

Her eyes filled with tears, but she didn't allow them to spill over. Instead, she summoned a laugh.

'You'd better go before I change my mind and beg you to stay,' she murmured huskily. 'Please, go, Phil. Go now...'

He nodded, turned and left without another word. He'd already pushed his luck, and it wouldn't have been fair to take further advantage of her vulnerability.

Driving home, Philip's feelings were mixed. He knew Susan's hints had helped to bring the situation between him and Megan to a head, but it had been coming on for a while now.

He might have been wiser to have kept silent for a bit longer, to have given them more time to have got to know each other—but theirs hadn't been a conventional affair. They had jumped several stages the night Megan had asked him to stay, and because of that Philip had gone beyond the point of no return.

He'd never expected to want to commit himself again, but now he knew it was what he wanted more than anything else. The need and the wanting was a physical ache, but he had given his word to Megan, and he had to keep it. No matter how much he wanted to move their relationship on, he had to be patient.

Because the thought of facing the future without her now was impossible.

CHAPTER EIGHT

MEGAN wasn't in her office the next afternoon. Philip knocked and looked in, then turned away. As he did so, he saw Staff Nurse Browne coming towards him along the corridor.

'If you're looking for Sister Hastings, she isn't here,' the young nurse said. 'She won't be coming in at all.'

'I thought she was working today?'

'She was but she called in sick. We've brought someone else in to cover for her for a few days.'

'Megan is ill?' Philip frowned. He felt panic strike at his stomach. He'd noticed those faint shadows beneath her eyes, but had put it down to lack of sleep. 'Do you know what was wrong with her?'

'I think she was in pain,' the staff nurse replied, frowning slightly. 'I heard Sister Morris telling her she should visit her own doctor, and that she wasn't to come back until she was feeling better.'

'I wonder if it was Susan's egg-nog,' Philip said, looking worried. 'I didn't have any myself, but sometimes raw eggs can—' He broke off, aware that he was thinking aloud, revealing too much of his private thoughts. He made himself smile. 'Thank you, Anne. Did you have a good Christmas yourself?'

'I was working,' Anne said shortly. 'Excuse me, I have to get back to the ward or Sister will be on the warpath.'

Philip frowned as she walked away. What had he said? He hadn't meant to upset her, but if Megan had been right about the young nurse having a crush on him, his polite inquiry, though kindly meant, might have confused and distressed her.

But he couldn't think about her any more. All he could think about at the moment was Megan herself. Was her illness a return of the malaria, or something else?

He turned and left the hospital at once, the staff nurse forgotten in his anxiety for Megan's welfare. Had she felt ill the previous evening—was that why she'd asked him not to stay?

Why hadn't she told him? Just what was wrong with her?

His mind kept going over and over their conversation. He was an inconsiderate fool not to have realised she was unwell. All he'd been thinking about was how much he cared for her—how much he wanted to stay. *His* feelings, *his* needs. And she had been in pain.

If she was seriously ill, he would never forgive himself!

The drive to Megan's cottage seemed to take for ever. As he pulled up outside, he saw that her car was still parked in the driveway. He jumped out of his own and went charging up the path, knocking at her door as if his life depended on it.

When she didn't answer it, he stepped back and looked up at the bedroom windows, calling her name.

'Megan—are you there? Are you all right? Do you need any help?' he shouted. 'Can I do anything for you?'

After a couple of minutes, the front door to the next house opened and Mrs Jones looked out at him. She came down the path towards him as he hesitated.

'She's not there, Dr Grant. A taxi came half an hour ago and took her away.'

'Do you know where it took her?' he asked, his voice fraught with worry. 'Did she say she was feeling ill—or where she was going?'

'She didn't say,' Mrs Jones replied, frowning slightly. 'I haven't spoken to her today. Yesterday she came round with a little present for me, but she seemed fine then.' The old lady hesitated, before venturing. 'I think sometimes she did have a bit of a stomach ache, but when I asked her once if she was all right she said it was just woman's trouble.'

'Woman's trouble...' Philip frowned, immediately alert. That could mean the time of the month, of course, but there were other things Megan might have meant. 'I'm a little concerned for her,' he said. 'If she comes home, will you let her know I was asking about her? I'm worried she might be unwell.'

'Of course, Doctor. If I see her, I'll go round and tell her you were here.'

Philip thanked her and went back to his car. He was thoughtful as he drove home. Something must have happened to have made Megan call in sick to work—but where had she gone? Why had she decided to go away without telling anyone?

Throughout the rest of the afternoon, as he was called out to the homes of various patients, his thoughts kept chasing themselves round and round. Where had Megan gone? Was she really ill, or had she called in sick just as an excuse to get away?

He would telephone the hospital later and discover whether or not they had heard from her, and he would keep ringing her cottage, but he had an awful feeling that she had run away. And he was very much afraid that something he'd said to her the previous evening might have precipitated her flight.

*　　*　　*

That evening, at home, Philip tried concentrating on the paperback thriller which had been one of Susan's presents to him the previous day, but it didn't help him to put Megan out of his mind, or stop him blaming himself for distressing her.

Why had she gone away so suddenly? Supposing she was really ill? There were a lot of bugs around at the moment, but something like that wouldn't have caused her to leave her home so mysteriously. He felt very concerned, and wished he could be with her, helping her through whatever was causing her pain.

Why hadn't he noticed before? To call himself a doctor and not realise that the woman who meant more to him than anyone else in the world was ill! He felt wretched, and guilty.

He had been blind...blind! He stood up and started pacing the room. It was no use, he couldn't sit here and do nothing. He'd rung Megan's cottage six times, but she wasn't answering even if she was there. Her machine was switched on and if he phoned much more the tape would run out!

He decided to drive down to the village again. He would try ringing her bell again, and if she wasn't there he would go up to the hospital and talk to some of the staff. Surely someone must know where Megan was likely to have gone.

Two hours later, Philip knew that he had drawn a blank. No one at the hospital had got close enough to Megan to know anything about her home life. He couldn't press too hard because they all gave him odd looks, as if he ought to know the answers to his own questions.

He should have done, of course. Philip cursed himself for not having pressed Megan for details of her home.

He thought her parents might have lived in London at one point, but he had no idea where or if they were still there.

The hospital in Manchester!

It came to him as he reached home again. He struck his forehead. Of course! There might be someone there who could tell him something about Megan's parents. At least, someone at the hospital might know where she was likely to have gone if she was feeling ill.

He reached for the phone, dialled Directory Enquiries and asked for the hospital's number.

It took a while before he managed to get through to anyone who seemed remotely interested in answering his questions. At first all he got was a blank refusal to discuss former staff.

'Look, I'm a friend of Sister Hastings,' Philip exploded after at last being put through to skeleton night staff in the personnel department. 'I think she may be ill and I'm trying to find out if there's anywhere she might have gone—to her parents' home, perhaps.'

'I'm sorry, sir. We're not permitted to give out personal details.'

'But you do know of her? You do know where she might have gone?'

'I do remember Sister Hastings, yes.'

'Then tell me where I might be able to get in touch with her.'

'I'm sorry, I can't do that.'

'I'm a doctor, for goodness sake! We're friends. She may be in trouble. I'm not a stalker or a murderer.'

'I'm sorry, sir,' the bored voice said again. 'We are not permitted—'

Philip slammed the phone down. He was well aware that he had been asking the woman to break the rules—

but what else could he do? He would go mad if he didn't hear from Megan!

He paced the room again, knowing he had played all his cards. There was nothing more he could do for the moment, except alert the police perhaps or start phoning all the hospitals in the area to see if she had been admitted.

He might even do that! Philip's hand was reaching for the phone when it suddenly rang. He snatched it up, breathless with worry.

'Megan—is that you?'

'No.' The voice was suspiciously like one he'd heard a little earlier. 'You don't know me, but I was Megan's friend when she worked in Manchester—'

'Do you know where she is?'

'No. Even if I did, I wouldn't tell you. But I have been in touch with her—'

'You've spoken to Megan? Where is she? What did she say?' Philip snatched eagerly at straws. 'Did you tell her I needed to talk to her?'

'She's all right. She did feel unwell earlier this morning, but she's fine now. She asked me to ring you to tell you not to worry. She's gone away for a few days. She'll ring you when she can so, please, don't worry—'

'You have her telephone number? Please, give it to me.'

'I'm sorry, I can't. Goodbye.'

'Please… Hello, are you there?' Philip frowned as the line went dead at the other end. He replaced his own receiver and dialled the recall number. An operator told him that the caller had withheld their own number and he cursed. He had made a stupid mess of all this! He was a damned idiot, but he was nearly going out of his mind.

Megan had obviously asked her friend to ring him and put his mind at ease concerning her health, but it hadn't helped him to understand why she'd run away.

Why would she do that? Unless he had done something to upset her. Philip cursed himself for pushing things the previous night. It was his own fault. He had known that Megan was still grieving, not yet ready to commit to a new relationship, so why had he brought up the subject of living together?

'Damn! Damn and blast it!'

Philip continued to pace the floor. He'd made too many mistakes, been too selfish, too aware of his own desires. No wonder Megan had run away from him.

Perhaps Susan would know something. His hand was reaching for the phone when it rang suddenly. It was a patient, asking for a home visit. Immediately, Philip switched into doctor mode.

'You say he's coughing, Mrs Roberts. Has he been sick?' Philip nodded as the anxious mother described her son's symptoms. 'You think he has a temperature—and a rash? Yes, you were right to call me. I'll come straight away. No, no, you haven't taken me away from anything important…'

He pushed his own problems to the back of his mind as he went out. He was making too much of this. Megan was able to look after herself. She was a very independent, capable woman. She wouldn't like him prying into her private life. She was probably annoyed with him for phoning her old hospital to ask if anyone could tell him where to contact her.

She was going to be away for a few days. When she did come back, it might be as well if he let things cool for a while. He might even try and book that skiing trip he'd been thinking about before Matthew's heart attack.

The child he had been called out to was suffering from chicken pox. Philip was able to set Mrs Roberts's mind at rest, driving home to find that there was a message from the hospital on the answerphone. He was needed to speak to one of his patients, who'd been taken worse during the day and was insisting on talking to Dr Grant.

He had several more calls during the night, and the next morning felt tired, drained and relieved that he had a free couple of days.

He spent the morning raking debris in the garden and making a bonfire. Every time the telephone rang he hoped it would be a call from Megan, but as the day wore on he realised she wasn't going to call him.

He had to stop worrying, he told himself. She wasn't ill—she just needed time for herself. He'd promised to give her that time, and he was being very foolish. Megan was a grown woman—she could take care of herself.

The day seemed to drag. He hardly knew what to do with himself. In the end he went for a long cross-country run to blow the cobwebs away. It was sheer punishment on such a cold day, but it did him the world of good. He was feeling better when he got back, and a suggestion from Henry that he should go round for a meal that evening found favour.

After all, what else could he do but wait until Megan decided to get in touch?

He and Susan took the children to London to see a couple of pantomimes. They stayed overnight in a nice hotel, and went shopping in the sales together.

Philip tried hard not to think about Megan. After all, she'd never promised anything...only to think about their relationship.

He was such a fool. Why hadn't he made his feelings clear from the start? He'd lost Megan once through carelessness, and he couldn't bear the idea that he might have done it again.

The days passed, and still there was no word from Megan. Philip found himself alternating between anger and anxiety. She was seldom out of his thoughts, at work or at home. Where was she—and why hadn't she phoned or written to let him know where she was? Had she been afraid he'd go charging after her? She couldn't trust him very much if she was afraid to tell him where she was staying.

That thought rankled, hurting his pride. He'd tried to be fair to her, but in the end he'd let his own feelings get out of hand. It was his own fault if Megan felt the need to be alone for a while. He accepted it, but it didn't help the ache in his heart.

Once when he came home to find the light flicking on the answerphone but no message, he wondered if she'd tried to ring him, especially when he tried to recall the number and was told it had been withheld. Why hadn't she left a message for him to ring her back—if it had been her?

Surely, if she cared, she would have wanted to talk to him? She must know that he was going through agony!

Sometimes, when he was angry, Philip cursed himself for caring. It might have been better if they'd never met. But he didn't really believe that. In his heart he knew that Megan was the best thing that had happened to him in a long time, and he was determined to hold onto her somehow.

She wasn't indifferent to him, he knew that instinctively. They were good together in bed, and in other ways—and they both needed a loving relationship. He had seen Megan with Susan's children, seen the wistfulness in her eyes when she talked of her sister's family, and he sensed that she was lonely. It was because of that he had spoken—because he wanted to protect her, to make her happy. He knew she was the right woman for him—but supposing he wasn't the man for her?

He could hardly bear to face up to that possibility. He had never felt this wretched in his life, and no amount of telling himself to be sensible and think of it from her point of view did a thing to help.

He was in love with Megan, more in love than he'd imagined possible, but he was trying not to let himself become too desperate. He still had his work and his family. He wouldn't allow himself to imagine how empty his life would be without Megan.

Matthew invited him to meet Fanny. They all had dinner together one night at a rather nice hotel, and Philip immediately liked her. She was older than he'd expected, but warm and very attractive, with dark hair and eyes and a slim figure.

'You needn't worry about Matt,' she told Philip when Matthew had gone to the cloakroom. 'I'm going to be looking after him now—and I'll make sure he eats properly and cuts down on the drinking.'

Matthew had invited her to move into his house, because it was bigger than hers, and it looked as if they were both pleased with the idea of living together.

'I'm not thinking of marriage at the moment,' Matt told him privately, 'but we'll see what happens. For the moment I feel lucky to have the chance to try again.'

'Just keep going to the fitness classes the hospital booked for you,' Philip said. 'I know it sounds odd to say you need exercise, but once you're over the worst of a heart attack that's exactly what you do need. Don't overdo it, of course. No squash for the time being. Plenty of walks and cycling, that's good, nothing too strenuous.'

'Just tell Fanny what you want me to do,' Matt said, and laughed wickedly. 'She has her own way of making sure I obey.'

Philip was naturally delighted that his friend had found someone to ease his loneliness, but it made him even more conscious of the emptiness of his own life without Megan.

On the morning of New Year's Eve he went up to the hospital. He hadn't rung Megan's home for a day or two now, because he was afraid she might not want to talk to him. If she'd gone away to think things through, she would surely have been in touch by now—that was if she wanted their relationship to continue.

Which meant that perhaps she'd decided to turn him down. The more he thought about the situation, the more he came to believe that he had overstepped the bounds, and that it was his fault she'd felt forced to go away.

So when he saw her car in the car park he felt as if a live wire had touched him. He wanted to head straight for her office, but controlled his impatience, making himself visit his patients first.

He had two patients on the medical ward. The first was a young man recovering from a severe bout of enterocolitis, which was a nasty inflammation of the mucous membrane of the intestine and colon. It had been touch and go for a while, but the patient seemed to be getting on well now and was sitting up, reading a magazine.

Philip had a chat with him and checked his chart, then passed on to an elderly man who had suffered a stroke the previous night.

He saw Megan making her rounds, but held back from

going over to her, checking his patient's chart and noting that he was still under sedation.

Megan had seen him, and was coming towards him.

'Good morning, Dr Grant,' she said in her most professional manner.

'Good morning, Sister,' Philip replied, continuing to study the chart. He had to follow her lead, to be calm and professional even though he wanted to grab her and force her to explain her actions. 'Mr Bull seems to be holding his own. I think his condition is satisfactory at this stage, don't you?'

'Yes, Doctor.' Megan hesitated. 'I only came back to work this morning. I believe he was admitted last night?'

Philip nodded. He gave her a long, thoughtful look. 'Are you better now?'

'Yes, thank you.' Megan seemed calm enough, though there was a faint flush in her cheeks. 'I'm sorry I haven't been in touch with you, but it was difficult—'

'Forget it,' Philip said quickly, his voice harsher than he'd intended. He was aware of conflicting emotions, foremost of which at that moment was probably anger. 'I don't own you, Megan. You're entitled to your independence. You've always made that clear.'

'Don't be angry,' she said in hushed tones, and her eyes seemed to reflect hurt. 'I'll explain this evening.'

'This evening...' Until that second Philip had forgotten Lady Rowen's party. He raised his eyebrows. 'You're still coming, then?'

'Yes, of course. I know it's important to you.'

'Other things are equally important, Megan.' He looked at her, his gaze narrowed and colder than he knew. This was Philip at his most intimidating, though he wasn't aware of it.

'I know. I'm sorry...' She looked uncomfortable, upset. 'I should have let you know what was happening. I wasn't thinking properly at first and then—'

'It doesn't matter,' he said, and his anger was gone as swiftly as it had come. She had every right to do whatever she saw fit. He gave her a cool, professional smile. 'I was simply worried about you. As long as you're all right, nothing else really matters.'

'Thank you...' She seemed to force the words out.

'I'll pick you up this evening, then. Seven-thirty sharp. Lady Rowen expects her dinner guests to be on time.' He glanced at his watch. 'I must go. We'll talk this evening?'

'Yes.' He thought she sounded subdued, but when he looked at her she gave no sign of being anything other than her usual efficient self. 'Yes, that's fine.'

Philip left her standing there. He was no longer angry. Instead, he had begun to feel a dull ache in his chest. Megan's reserve hadn't been encouraging, and he was unable to convince himself that she thought of him as anything other than a colleague and a friend.

CHAPTER NINE

PHILIP finished afternoon surgery and went out to his car. His list had been a light one for a change. He'd examined a man with lower back and groin pain, and had referred him to the hospital for an X-ray. It was possible that it was a recurrence of kidney stones, the patient having suffered from them some years earlier.

'It may be a while before you get to see a consultant,' Philip had warned his patient. 'There's a long waiting list for urinary clinics. In the meantime, drink plenty of water. If you get sharp pain, ring the surgery immediately and we might be able to have you admitted for emergency treatment. If there is a stone, it will probably need to be shattered, a procedure grandly called extra-corporeal shock-wave lithotripsy! The treatment isn't usually too painful, though there is a sensation of your skin being flicked vigorously with an elastic band—it lasts between thirty and sixty minutes.'

'When can I have it done, Doctor? I'm feeling most uncomfortable at the moment,' the patient asked. 'Shall I need longer than a day off work?'

'You may experience a dull ache in your kidney afterwards,' Philip said. 'Some people do feel more pain than others, but you'll be given painkillers and antibiotics to take afterwards. Hopefully, you won't need to be off work for more than a couple of days.'

Philip had arranged for urine and blood tests, but there wasn't much else he could do for the moment, except provide painkilling tablets. If there was a stone it might possibly pass, and that could be very unpleasant for the sufferer.

His own mood was sombre as he drove home. He wasn't particularly looking forward to the party that evening. It would be a formal affair and he'd always thought of it as more of a duty than a pleasure—the pleasure would have come from having Megan as his partner. Now he was conscious of a shadow hanging over the evening, making him uneasy.

His proposal on Christmas Day had put Megan under so much pressure that she'd needed to run away from him. She'd clearly not been ill—that had merely been an excuse.

Philip found that hurtful, and it also made him feel guilty. He would very much regret it if she felt she had to move on because of his attentions.

Philip made up his mind to be very careful that evening. He would be friendly but keep his distance. He could no longer pretend, even to himself, that his feelings for Megan were anything less than love, but if it turned out that she wanted to end their affair, he would have no choice but to let her go.

She'd said she wanted to talk, and he was prepared for the worst. He would do his best to be understanding and not pressure her in any way.

He was wearing formal evening dress as he drove to Megan's cottage that evening, timing his arrival for exactly seven-thirty, which would give them a few minutes to talk before they had to leave for the party.

Pulling up outside Megan's home, he frowned as he saw there were no lights on inside. Her car was in the drive as usual, but he had an odd feeling that she wasn't at home. He frowned as he went up to the door and rang the bell. There was no answer and he rang it again several times, then stepped back to look up at the bedroom windows.

Where was she? Philip frowned, beginning to feel very annoyed. Megan couldn't have forgotten their arrangement. It wasn't possible. She'd been so sure when she'd spoken to him earlier that day. Surely she hadn't run off again? What possible reason could she have for doing so? He hadn't done or said anything to distress her. In fact, he believed he'd been completely professional that morning, even aloof.

He rang the bell again but, not wanting to bring Mrs Jones to her door, didn't call out this time. It really was too bad of Megan! If she'd told him that morning that she didn't want to come, he might have made other arrangements. He could at least have let Lady Rowen know so that she could make some arrangement of her own.

Philip glanced at his watch. Had Megan popped out for a few minutes? It was chilly, standing about, so he went back to his car. He picked up his mobile phone, making a call to the hospital to check whether Megan was still on duty, though that was unlikely as her car was in the drive.

'May I speak to Sister Hastings, please?'

'I'm sorry. Sister Hastings left an hour ago. May I take a message, sir?'

Philip cut the call, then rang Megan's home. The answerphone clicked in and he swore. It really was too bad of her to do this again. He could only suppose that she had gone off somewhere in a taxi, just as she had on Boxing Day.

Well, he couldn't waste time waiting here! He would simply have to attend the party and apologise to Lady Rowen!

'You don't need to apologise,' Lady Rowen said, smiling at him as he arrived a few minutes late. 'I understand perfectly. I believe Sister Hastings has been unwell recently, which is a great shame. She has been a useful addition to our staff at the Chestnuts, and we shall miss her if she decides to leave us.'

'I'm sorry, I don't quite understand,' Philip replied with a frown. 'Is there any question of her leaving?'

'I think there is some possibility of her leaving,' his hostess said. 'I am not perfectly sure what the situation is—but do come and join the others, Dr Grant. I believe you know everyone…'

Philip nodded and followed her into the rather warm and slightly overcrowded sitting room. He was conscious of feeling irritated. Just what had Lady Rowen meant about Megan leaving the Chestnuts? Had she already made up her mind to go, without telling him?

He felt sick and shaken by the possibility.

Why had she stood him up this evening? She'd known it was important. Perhaps that was why… Philip dismissed the idea as unworthy. Megan wouldn't have done it deliberately.

He'd refused to go to a wedding with her, but that had been a long time ago and she wouldn't have done this as a way of getting her revenge on him. No! He was certain Megan hadn't done this out of spite—and yet why had she done it? She could have picked up the phone, for goodness' sake! What on earth was she playing at? Surely he hadn't done anything to deserve this sort of treatment?

Philip had never known an evening to drag as this one did, or himself to have felt so much out of sorts with everyone around him. It took all his strength of purpose not to turn around and leave five minutes after he'd arrived, but gradually, as his first irritation passed, it was replaced by a cold anger.

Megan had gone off on Boxing Day without a word, leaving him in a kind of limbo. Now she'd done it again, and it wasn't good enough. He'd been prepared to accept that it had been his fault the first time, but this was inexcusable. If she'd decided she didn't want to come to the party, she might at least have let him know. It wouldn't have taken her two minutes to pick up the phone!

Anger made it possible for him to get through the party, but he left before midnight, pleading pressure of work.

'I had hoped you might stay for my announcement,' Lady Rowen said as he went to say goodbye to her, 'but I shall tell you my decision since you have worked so tirelessly for the fund. I have given the Chestnuts a cheque to enable the unit to be finished—and set up an endowment fund for its future support. It is my hope that we shall be able to employ sufficient staff to run it in the way we had all hoped. And I am hoping that you will sit on the board, of course.'

'You're very generous,' Philip said. 'I really can't thank you enough for all you've done.'

It was all that he had hoped for and more, much more. Philip wondered why he felt no elation as he drove home. Only a few weeks ago Lady Rowen's generosity would have given him a terrific boost, but now he felt only mild pleasure that the children's unit's future was secure for the foreseeable future.

He would probably begin to realise how marvellous her gesture was tomorrow, Philip thought as he let himself into his cottage. At the moment, all he was conscious of was an emptiness, a feeling akin to despair.

As he walked into the hall, he saw that the light was flashing on his answerphone. He picked it up, frowning as he heard a muffled sound and then a receiver being replaced with a clatter.

Could it have been Megan? Had she tried to phone him earlier? Surely she would have left a message?

He glanced at his watch. It was nearly midnight. Should he telephone her now? For a moment he was tempted, then he shook his head and went upstairs. He had no desire to see in the New Year. He could see no prospect of the kind of future he'd hoped might await him with Megan as his wife.

Philip made no attempt to ring Megan the next morning. By breaking their arrangement for the previous evening, she had made her feelings clear. He had his answer and, painful as it was to accept, he realised there was no alternative.

Had he been able, he would have avoided seeing Megan for a few days, but during the morning he received a call from the hospital to say that his stroke patient had made a good recovery overnight and had asked to see him personally.

Philip went in that afternoon. It had cost him some sleepless hours the previous night, but he had reached a decision. If he was forced to speak to Megan, he would be cool and detached and leave things as they were. There was plainly no point in making things awkward for her, and he had no wish to drive her away from the Chestnuts.

She had behaved badly over the party, but it was his fault for having tried to force her into committing herself to a relationship she plainly did not want. Somehow he must make her believe that he was as indifferent as she so obviously was herself.

He found his patient sitting up in bed, seemingly much recovered. He had a slight speech impediment, which Philip assured him would in time respond to treatment with the physiotherapist, but no paralysis of arms or legs.

'I've been lucky, haven't I?' he said. 'I might have died.'

'This was only a slight one,' Philip said. 'We shall be putting you on half an aspirin a day and keeping an eye on you, Mr Bull, but I'm glad to say you've been lucky.'

'It's my wife I'm worried about,' the man said. 'She shouldn't be left on her own, Doctor. She forgets to take her insulin when I'm not there. I wonder if perhaps you could arrange for the nurse to go in and see she's all right?'

'Yes, I'm sure we can do that,' Philip replied. 'I'll call in on her myself this afternoon, and I'll arrange for a nurse to go in every morning and help her with the injection.'

'You've set my mind at rest,' the elderly man said. 'I don't know what my poor Bessie would do if anything happened to me.'

'Don't worry about it,' Philip said. 'We'll keep an eye on her, Mr Bull. We are always aware of patients who need us, and in a small community like this we know when things are going wrong.'

'There aren't many around like you, Dr Grant,' the patient said, grabbing his hand and holding it tightly. 'It's a gift, the gift of loving your fellow beings. Folk say as you're cold and distant at times, but I reckon it's them what can't see beyond the end of their noses...'

Philip was touched. He felt quite emotional as he left

the ward. He had decided not to try and see Megan, but she came out as he was about to pass her office.

'May I speak with you, please?'

'I'm not sure that would be a good idea,' Philip said, all his good intentions sent flying as he felt a surge of anger. 'What happened last night, Megan? I came to pick you up but you weren't there.'

'I know…' She flushed. 'Please, come into my office. I want to apologise.'

Philip followed her inside. He wasn't in a mood of reconciliation. Perhaps it was unfair, but he was damned angry. He stared at Megan, his expression hard and ungiving.

'I was prepared to accept it was my fault the first time,' he said, not waiting for her to begin, 'but you could have told me yesterday morning you didn't want to go to the party. It was annoying for Lady Rowen to have her table arrangements spoiled at the last moment. She was very good about it, but it was awkward.'

'Yes, I know it was wrong of me,' Megan said. She avoided looking at him. 'I'm very sorry for what happened, Phil—last night and before—'

'As I said, I understood the first time,' he went on, too angry to really listen to what she was saying. 'I realise that was my fault, though I still think you might have telephoned to say you were all right—'

'I did ask someone to ring you—'

'Only after I had been going mad, trying to find you,' Philip said. 'I know it was because of me that you went—and I must apologise for that, of course. It was only a suggestion that we might have got on rather well together, but I completely understand that you—'

'No,' she said in a whisper. 'No, you don't understand at all.'

'Then tell me,' he invited, staring at her hard. 'Don't play games with me, Megan. I thought we were both adults.'

'Yes, of course we are,' she said, her head going up. Her eyes flashed with pride. 'I understand that you're angry, Phil. I should have told you I was going away, but…'

'But what?'

She shook her head, as if she couldn't bear all this. 'It really doesn't matter, does it? I'm sorry I caused a problem for you last night, but I don't suppose it caused huge waves. I dare say Lady Rowen forgave you—you are her blue-eyed boy, aren't you? Everyone says—'

'Be damned to that! If it comes to that, Megan, everyone says you were asked to leave your last hospital…'

'That's not true,' she replied, her face white with shock. 'I left because I refused to cover up for someone—a doctor who made a mistake by prescribing a massive overdose for a child. I refused to administer it and asked another doctor to check the prescription. But I wasn't liked because of it. The doctor concerned made life unbearable for me, but I wouldn't give in to his bullying so I left and took a job abroad.' Her eyes flashed with anger. 'I thought you didn't listen to gossip? If you'd asked me, I would have told you the truth. I think it's disgusting that you should even think I had done something that would call for my dismissal. Just because people talk… But you're so unfair! You never try to see things from my side.'

'I don't give a damn what anyone says,' Philip said, and swore furiously, because he knew he was wrong, and could have cut his tongue out for throwing the accusation at her. He had only meant to show her that there was no good to be gained from listening to the tongue-waggers. But he was angry with her now and couldn't help hitting back. 'If that's your attitude, Megan, I don't think we have much to say to one another.'

'No, I don't suppose we have,' she replied. She lifted her head once more, giving him a look to match his own. 'It won't bother you for much longer. I shall be leaving at the end of the week.'

'That suits me just fine,' Philip said, and walked out before he lost his temper completely.

'Dr Grant…'

Someone called to him as he left the hospital but he didn't look back. At that moment he wasn't fit company for anyone.

Driving home, he calmed down a little, realising that he'd made a bit of an idiot of himself back there. It was unusual for Philip to lose his temper, but he hadn't been able to control himself when Megan had seemed to dismiss what had happened as being of little importance.

Didn't she know how he felt about her? Didn't she realise what it had done to him when she'd run away? She had to know—which meant she didn't care, didn't want him to care for her.

God, that hurt! He felt as if someone had stuck pins all over him. It was just as well she was leaving. If he'd been forced to see her every time he visited the medical ward…

Megan was leaving. The realisation really began to hit home only after he was back at the cottage. After this week he would probably never see her again, never hear her voice or see her smile…

He sank down in a chair, feeling closer to weeping than he ever had in his life. He loved her so much, couldn't even begin to think of what life would be like when she was no longer around.

He was a damned fool! What was he going to do?

There was nothing he could do, short of crawl. He would do even that if he thought it would help to win her back, but she didn't want him—had never wanted more than a casual affair. She probably didn't trust him, didn't believe he could really care for anyone. And that was his own fault. If only he hadn't refused to go to that wedding all those years ago…but they had both been so young then. He hadn't realised how much he'd cared for Megan until she'd left him, and this time it hurt even more.

Yet there was very little he could do if she didn't want him. He would just have to accept that and get on with his life, though it was going to be hard. He wasn't sure he could do it, not without going away somewhere. He might have to look for a different job.

The telephone rang. Philip reached for it, hoping against hope.

'Phil…' Susan was at the other end. 'What's this I hear about Megan leaving the Chestnuts? You haven't quarrelled with her, have you?'

'We did have a bit of an argument this morning. She stood me up for Lady Rowen's party. I was annoyed.'

'Well, if what I've been hearing is right, she may have had good reason,' Susan said. 'Didn't you ask her why she didn't go to the party, Phil?'

'Sort of…I was angry…'

'So you just chewed her head off. No wonder she's had enough of you. You're in the wrong, Phil, and I think you should apologise.'

'What have you heard?' Philip asked, not bothering to argue. He knew he was the biggest fool ever.

'Something about her needing to have an operation, but I don't know if that's true. Someone heard her talking to Mrs Jones in the village shop but I'm not sure it's right. It might be just gossip.'

'Who told you that?'

'No, I'm not going to tell you, Phil. It wouldn't be right. I was told in confidence.' Susan hesitated. 'Maybe Megan doesn't know how you feel about her, Philip.'

'What do you mean?' Philip asked. 'I asked her if she would like to move in with me or get married—whatever she was comfortable with.'

'Did tell her you were in love with her?'

'No…probably not. I was trying not to frighten her.'

'Then perhaps you should tell her,' Susan suggested. 'If I were you, Phil, I'd tell her as soon as you can. Before it's too late…'

CHAPTER TEN

No matter how distressed he may have felt personally, Philip wasn't about to neglect his work. He kept his word to his patient by calling on Mrs Bull on his way to the surgery, spending half an hour with her and persuading her that it would be no trouble at all for a nurse to visit every morning to make sure she took her insulin.

'I'm sorry to be so much trouble to you, Doctor,' the elderly lady said. 'It's just that I'm so forgetful these days. My husband looks after me when he's home, but while he's away...' She shook her head and sighed. 'It's so silly of me.'

'It's no trouble for the nurse,' Philip assured her. 'And Mr Bull will soon be home himself. He's getting on very well.'

Arriving at the surgery, Philip discovered he had a heavy list to get through. He tackled it with his usual attention, finding that the ache in his heart eased a little as he tried to solve his patients' problems.

Perhaps Susan was right, he thought as he finished for the evening. Perhaps he ought to tell Megan he loved her—but surely she knew? It must have been obvious. Unless he did give the appearance of being aloof, a little distant. He had never seen himself that way, but he was beginning to realise that others might. Megan had said something similar to him once. Something about him being elusive.

All those years ago, when they'd dated as students, Megan had hinted that he hadn't been really interested in her. Was she still thinking the same way? That he was only interested in her as a casual companion, someone to take out occasionally and sleep with when it suited him? She couldn't have thought that, could she? Surely she must have realised how much she meant to him? He had played it cool for a while so as not to rush her... Good grief, he must be a better actor than he'd thought! He must have succeeded too well.

Philip frowned as he locked the surgery and went out to his car. At least he could apologise to Megan for his show of bad temper...if she was still speaking to him, that was, and if she was in. She'd said she was leaving the Chestnuts at the end of the week—he just hoped she hadn't decided to leave earlier than planned.

As he drove towards her cottage, Philip knew he couldn't let things stay the way they were. Even if Megan didn't want to marry him, surely they could still be friends?

He knew he was clutching at straws. He mustn't hope for too much, but he thought he could bear their parting a little more easily if she forgave him for causing her grief.

He slowed the car to stop at the front of her house, sitting in his seat for a few moments after he'd turned the engine off. Megan's car was in the drive, but that didn't mean anything. Even if she was in, it was going to be a painful experience, but he couldn't just leave it—he had to speak to Megan. He had to tell her what was in his heart, to apologise for hurting her.

He walked up to the front door, then took a deep breath and rang the bell. The door opened almost at once, as if she had known he was there. He stared at her, noticing that she looked pale, strained.

'May I come in?' he asked. 'I want to apologise for

the way I behaved this morning. I shouldn't have lost my temper. I said things I didn't mean because I was angry and upset. Terrible things! Please, forgive me. I'm sorry if I hurt you.'

She stood back, allowing him to enter, but didn't say anything. Of course, she must be furious with him. He couldn't blame her for that—he was angry with himself for hurting her. In her sitting room Philip stood in front of the fire, holding his hands to the flames and wondering how to begin, then he heard an odd sound behind him.

Turning, he caught a glimpse of something in Megan's face. She was fighting her emotions, trying not to give way to tears, but it was obvious that she was suffering. He took a step towards her, catching her hands. Then he realised that she was shaking.

'Are you ill?' he asked, suddenly concerned. 'What's wrong, Megan?' He looked at her face, seeing the shadows beneath her eyes. She'd been crying earlier that evening—all the signs were there—but his professional instincts told him there was more to this than their quarrel. 'You're unwell, aren't you?' She nodded, then tore her hands from his and turned her back on him. 'Is that the reason you didn't come to the door last night?' He suddenly knew the truth. 'You were here, weren't you? But you wouldn't answer your door—why?'

'I was feeling shocked and I just couldn't face you. I simply couldn't go to a party, feeling the way I did,' Megan said in a choked voice. 'You said it was your fault that I went away at Christmas, Phil, but that wasn't quite true. I did need to think about what you'd said—but that wasn't my only reason.'

Philip turned her gently to face him. 'Sit down,' he said. 'Tell me what's upsetting you—and don't pretend there isn't anything, Megan. I think we owe each other the truth, if nothing else, don't you? Something's wrong, isn't it?'

She nodded, then breathed deeply. 'I had been having some pain for a while, even before I came back to England. I should have gone to the doctor ages ago, but I suppose I'm a coward. The trouble is, when you think you know what might be wrong...'

'Yes, I know.' Philip smiled at her as she faltered. 'Some of my patients read about terrible illnesses in the paper and then think they've got whatever it is they've been reading about. It's even worse for someone who has to deal with very sick people all the time.'

'The pain got worse just before Christmas,' Megan said. 'I kept promising myself I'd go to a doctor, but I never seemed to have time...a weak excuse, I know. I suppose I was afraid to face the truth.'

'You thought it might be cancer? Because of Simon?'

He saw the grief and fear in her eyes, and his heart wrenched. She had been going through so much and he had known nothing about it, done nothing to help her. He had quarrelled with her over a wretched party!

'A friend of mine had similar pain. She had a cyst on her ovary. It was malignant and she had to have an Oophorosalpingectomy, which meant, of course, that it decreased her chances of having children. It isn't impossible that she'll have a child, but she's been trying for a long time without success, and I know she feels pretty desperate about the situation.'

Philip nodded. The removal of an ovary and a Fallopian tube was not helpful to women who hoped to have children, although as long as one ovary remained the chances remained reasonable.

'Yes, I see,' Philip said. He looked at Megan thought-

fully. 'Did you see a doctor while you were away?' She
nodded. 'And what did he say, my darling?' He reached
for her hand, holding it gently, tenderly. 'Whatever it
was, let me help you through this. Please, Megan?
Please, don't refuse my help.'

'Oh, Philip,' Megan said in a choking voice. 'I've
been so miserable. I went away, to my parents', to think
about what you asked me on Christmas Day, and my
mother saw I was in pain almost at once. She made me
go to the doctor, and I was admitted into a private clinic
immediately for X-rays and tests.' She took a deep
breath, her face pale. 'After Simon…she was terrified I
might have cancer, too. There is definitely a cyst. They
aren't sure whether it's malignant or not, but I'm booked
in to have it removed next week.' She choked back a
sob. 'I should have telephoned you or written, but I just
couldn't, Phil.'

'Couldn't you trust me?' he asked, looking deep into
her eyes. 'I wish you'd told me, Megan. I thought you'd
run away from me.'

She shook her head, smiling mistily. 'Why would I
want to do that?' she asked in a husky voice. 'You're
the best thing that has ever happened to me, Phil.'

'Am I?'

'Oh, yes,' she said softly, and now she was smiling,
her eyes warm and filled with something that made
Philip catch his breath. 'I was so unhappy the night I
asked you to stay with me,' Megan confessed. 'I had
just lost my brother and I was still a little raw, still a
little wary… There had been someone else I'd thought
I loved. We broke up just before I went to stay with my
sister. I was too raw, too hurt to want another relationship for a long time, but when I saw you again it was…'

'What was it, my darling?' he prompted, kissing the

palm of her hand. 'For me it was like coming out into the sunshine after a very long winter…'

'Oh, Phil…' She laughed, a rueful look in her eyes. 'I had a terrible crush on you when you were at Guy's. You seemed to treat me as just one of the crowd, and I was so in love with you. I was furious that you wouldn't come to that wedding. It took me a long time to forget you. After I heard you'd married Helen, I went a bit wild for a while, had a few affairs that were going no-where. Then two years ago I met Richard…'

'And you fell in love?'

'Yes, I did love him,' she admitted. 'He was so clever, such a brilliant man—and he said I made him feel young. He was several years older than me. He told me he was divorced, and I believed him…but it wasn't true. He was still living with his wife, still married. He lied to me—all the time we were together he lied to me. I felt such a fool, so angry at what he'd done. And I was having a miserable time at work because of not covering up for the doctor I told you about. So I finished the affair and went to my sister…then I was ill and I had to come back.'

'Oh, my darling. That was terrible for you, the way he lied to you, hurt you. You never suspected the truth?'

'No. Afterwards I realised I should have suspected something, but he swore he loved me, that he wanted to be with me. At first I thought it was just his work that kept him away so much. He travelled a lot in his business.' Megan's eyes reflected her sadness and her pain at being deceived and betrayed. 'In my heart I began to wonder why he was never with me over the holidays,' she said, blinking hard. 'But until his wife came to my flat I never knew…'

'Is that why you were angry with me when I danced

with Anne Browne, because you thought I was treating her the way Richard had treated you? Played with your feelings?'

'I did wonder.' Megan nodded. 'For a moment it all came back to me—the humiliation and the pain. Afterwards, I realised I was misjudging you, and it made me think about us, Phil. When Susan kept dropping hints and then you asked me to think about us getting together…maybe getting married.'

'Susan's hints had nothing to do with it,' Philip said. 'I had been thinking about you a lot. I was just worried about upsetting you. I sensed you'd been hurt and I was afraid of rushing you.'

She reached up to touch his cheek. 'You're so considerate,' she said. 'Such a loving man, Phil. For a while I wasn't sure. You seemed a little distant, not like the medical student I had been so in love with, but when I saw how you were with Matt I knew I still loved you. Perhaps I never stopped loving you.'

'Then…why didn't you contact me while you were away?' he asked. 'If it wasn't that you wanted to end the affair? I don't understand, Megan. You must know how much I want us to be together. Why did you just disappear like that?'

She twisted her hands in her lap, her face pale. 'Don't you see, Phil?' she asked, glancing up suddenly. 'I know you feel something for me. I know we're good together. But you asked me to be your partner because you want a family. If what I have is malignant, they may have to take the ovary away. It might be impossible for me to have a child…and that wouldn't be fair to you, my dearest.' She bit her lip. 'That's why I couldn't face you last night. I didn't get the results of my tests until yesterday afternoon. When they told me…' She caught her breath. 'It would spoil everything…'

'You foolish girl,' Philip said softly. He took her face in his hands, making her look at him, and smiled. Then he kissed her very gently on the mouth. 'Don't you know that all I really care about is you, my love? I have been going mad these past few days, worrying about whether you were ill, thinking that I had frightened you away, blaming myself for rushing you. Yes, I would like children—but I'm not sure I can live at all without you.'

'Oh, Phil…' A single tear slid from the corner of her eye. He wiped it away with his thumb. 'I do love you. I fell in love with you years ago, and when we met again it was almost as if the years between had never been.'

'I wish they hadn't,' he said fervently. 'I wish I'd gone to the wedding with you. I wish there had been no Helen and no Richard. I wish I could take all the pain away, my darling love. It was all my fault for being such an arrogant idiot and refusing to go to your brother's wedding.'

'No,' she said, smiling as she touched his cheek again. 'It wasn't all your fault. You offered to come to the evening reception. I should have accepted that…but perhaps we were both just too young.'

'I wish I could turn the clock back…take away all the pain for you.'

'It doesn't hurt any more,' she whispered. 'I stopped caring for Richard a long time ago. I was upset when my brother died, and it made me reach out to you. I realised after we made love that I had never known another man I cared for as much as you, but it frightened me.'

'Because you thought I only wanted an affair?'

She nodded. 'Everyone told me that you—'

'No more of that, my love.' He touched a finger to her lips. 'Everyone was wrong, Megan. I wanted you from the moment I saw you that day at the Chestnuts. It took me a little longer to understand my true feelings towards you—but I know now that I want to be with you always.'

'But that doesn't change things, Phil. You love children so much and I may not—'

He silenced her with a kiss that left them both shaken and breathless. 'I love kids,' he said when he let her go at long last. 'But I love you more than my life, Megan. I haven't been able to face the thought of living without you. I was beginning to think I would have to leave the village and go away somewhere. I don't think I could have coped with living here, passing this cottage every day…knowing I had driven you away with my selfish needs.'

'You—selfish?' Megan looked at him in wonder. 'How could you think that? You may sometimes appear distant to those who don't know you, but underneath you are the most unselfish, the most loving, giving man I have ever known.'

'Then promise me you won't do anything silly again,' Philip said, caressing her face with his fingertips. 'Promise me you will never run away from me again, that you will always share whatever is causing you pain.'

'I promise,' she said, reaching up to kiss him on the lips. 'Are you sure you want to—?'

She got no further. Philip's kiss took her breath away, and afterwards all she could do was smile and lean her head into his shoulder.

'It's so nice to be taken care of,' she said. 'I've never had anyone to worry about me before, Phil. I think I rather like it.'

'You must tell me if I fuss too much,' he said with a rueful grin. 'I do tend to fuss over those I love.'

'But you love them,' Megan said. 'You give so much love, Phil. Not just to your family, but to your patients and friends.'

'Someone else told me that recently,' he said, his mouth quirking. 'He said it was a gift—a gift I gave to everyone. If I do, it's quite unconscious. I'm just a very ordinary chap, Megan. I try to do my best, but it's not always easy and I fail all the time…'

'No, you don't,' she said, and kissed him. 'You do all you can for everyone, and no one can ask more than that.'

Philip smiled and nodded, then kissed her forehead. 'So when is this op taking place, then?'

'Next week—Tuesday morning,' she said. 'My mother insisted on paying for me to go privately.'

'If she hadn't, I would have,' Philip said. 'I want this thing sorted out, Megan, not because I'm concerned whether or not we can make babies—that will happen if and when it does—but because I shan't rest until I know you're safe.'

'If it helps, my doctor says he thinks it's just a cyst,' Megan said, 'but he won't be certain until after the operation.'

'Then we'll just have to wait and pray, won't we?' He held her close, his lips moving against her hair, her eyes closed. He knew that her chances were good, whatever the outcome of the operation, but there was always a risk and he couldn't bear the thought of losing her. 'It will be all right, my love. I'll be there until you go into Theatre, and I'll be waiting for you when you come out again. Whatever happens, we'll be together for the rest of our lives. And as soon as you're better, we'll be mar-

ried...' He looked down at her. 'You are going to con-
found all the gossips and marry me—aren't you? No
matter what the result on Tuesday?'

'Yes,' she said, and snuggled up to him. 'Yes, please,
Phil.'

He bent his head and kissed her. 'Well, I suppose I
ought to go and let you get some rest.'

'Are you on call tonight?'

'No, but you aren't feeling well...'

'Please, don't go,' she whispered. 'Stay with me, Phil.
Hold me, kiss me...make love to me.'

'Aren't you in pain? You can't want me to make love
to you at the moment.'

'It doesn't hurt all the time,' she said, her cheeky
smile peeping through. 'I just want to be with you, to
have you near me. Is that foolish of me?'

'No, of course not,' he replied. 'It's the way I feel all
the time. We can be together, darling, of course we can.
I can touch you, kiss you...'

'I shan't break if you love me,' Megan said, a wicked
look in her eyes. 'I want you, Phil. I want to make up
for all the lost nights we ought to have had all these
years...'

'My darling girl,' he whispered huskily. 'Don't worry,
we're going to have years together. We're going to have
everything we ever wanted. I promise you.'

Philip glanced at his watch. It was the second time he'd
looked at it in two minutes. Megan had been taken into
Theatre ages ago. What was going on? Why were they
taking so long? Had they found more than they'd expected? Was it cancer?

He'd never been through such agony. If Megan's condition turned out to be worse than they'd thought... He

jumped to his feet as he saw the surgeon coming towards him.

'Dr Grant?'

'Yes?' Philip's heart seemed to nearly stop. He understood how his patients felt when they had to wait for loved ones to come out of Theatre. 'How is she? Was it malignant?'

'As you know, Megan was most insistent that she didn't want the ovary removed unless we found definite evidence of cancer…'

'Yes. I couldn't overrule her on that, though we both knew it could mean further surgery.'

'We removed the cyst only,' the surgeon went on. 'The damage to the ovary was therefore minimal, and I'm glad to say that I believe it's not malignant. We shall have to do the usual biopsy on the tissue removed to be certain, of course, but I've done enough of these things to have a gut feeling and it's my feeling that Megan's ovaries are perfectly healthy. I see no reason why she shouldn't have that baby she's so keen on.'

'Thank God,' Philip said, and a surge of relief went over him. 'It means an awful lot to Megan—partly for my sake, because she knows I want a family, but for her own sake as well.' He offered his hand to the surgeon. 'I can't thank you enough.'

'I'm pleased we had the right result,' the surgeon said, grinning at him. 'It's hellish when you have to give bad news—especially to colleagues.'

Philip nodded. 'I feel as if I've been through a wringer,' he said. 'When can I see her?'

'Hang on for half an hour or so, and a nurse will come to take you through to her.'

Philip thanked him again. He paced the floor, overcome with relief, then went to greet Megan's mother who had been down to the canteen to fetch a cup of tea for them both.

'It's good news,' he said, taking the plastic cup she offered. 'Megan is fine and it looks as if the cyst was harmless.'

'Thank goodness for that,' Mrs Hastings said. 'Can we see her?'

'In a little while.' Philip smiled at her. 'Will you hang on in case they call us? I want to get something from the car. I daren't bring it in before now—in case things went wrong.'

Mrs Hastings nodded. 'I'll wait for you,' she said. 'I'm so glad Megan had you to see her through this, Phil. Since her brother's cancer was diagnosed, I've been worried about her. I wanted to see her happy. It's what I've always wanted—a happy, settled life for my girl.'

Philip kissed her cheek, then went down in the lift to the car park. He unlocked the boot of his car, taking out the basket of flowers, the small jeweller's box—and the huge white teddy bear.

People looked at the bear as he carried it back upstairs, smiling and nodding at him. He thought he was probably grinning like a Cheshire cat, but he couldn't stop himself.

'They say we can go in,' Mrs Hastings greeted him as he joined her. 'You go first, Phil. I'll come in a few minutes.'

'Thank you,' he said. 'You're going to be a great mother-in-law!'

Philip's heart was racing as he went into the little room where Megan was recovering. She was propped up against a pile of pillows with her eyes closed, but she opened them as he bent to kiss her cheek, smiling at him a little groggily, still half-asleep.

'Hi…' she said as he presented her with the flowers. 'They are lovely, Phil. You spoil me.'

'Not as much as I'm going to,' he promised, then sat the teddy on the end of her bed. 'This one isn't for you. You can keep him for the time being…just until we have our first child. And we're going to have children, my darling. I promise you.'

'Oh, Phil…' Tears appeared in her eyes, sliding down her cheeks, and he sat on the side of the bed, then bent his head to kiss her tenderly on the lips. 'It was all right, then?'

'Yes, of course it was,' he said, smiling at her. 'Didn't I tell you it would be?'

'I wasn't sure…'

'It had to be,' Philip said. 'You deserve happiness, my darling. And I intend to see that you get it.' He opened the little jeweller's box, showing her the large diamond solitaire engagement ring and a platinum wedding band. 'I hope you like these, but we could always change them…'

'No, never,' she said, and smiled up at him. 'I think it's very romantic that you bought them for me. I like strong, masterful men, Phil. I enjoy being treated like Dresden china.'

'Do you?' Philip's brows went up. 'I seem to remember you are a very independent lady…'

'There are times to be independent,' Megan said, 'and times when it's good to know there's a broad shoulder waiting if you need it.'

'It will always be there,' he said, then his eyes began to twinkle. 'I've been thinking…'

'What are you up to? I know that look.' Megan gave him a challenging smile. 'What are you thinking now?'

'Well, as my wife, you'll belong to the village,' Philip

said. 'There's another challenge match for the darts team
in the spring. I've been asked to organise it, but in the
village hall this time—a grand affair with raffles and
tombola and all manner of similar delights. I thought we
might get competitors to dress up as either Maid Marian
or Robin Hood. I rather fancy you as a Robin Hood.'
He chuckled as he saw her expression. 'I was thinking,
with you on our side the village team can't lose.'

'I think that's why you asked me to marry you,'
Megan said, and laughed.

'Yes, of course,' Philip replied, looking at her with
love in his eyes. 'Why else?'

MILLS & BOON®

Makes any time special™

Mills & Boon publish 29 new titles
every month. Select from...

Modern Romance™   Tender Romance™

Sensual Romance™

Medical Romance™   Historical Romance™

MAT2

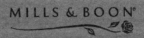

MILLS & BOON®

Medical Romance™

JUST A FAMILY DOCTOR *by Caroline Anderson*

Audley Memorial

Allie Baker's new job as Staff Nurse at Audley Memorial Hospital brought her back into contact with Senior Houseman Mark Jarvis. Love blossomed until she found out he was going to become a GP—a profession she had sworn never to marry into…

ONE AND ONLY *by Josie Metcalfe*

First of a Trilogy

The victim of a childhood custody battle, Cassie Mills had vowed never to be second best. But Dr Luke Thornton needed her help to fight for custody of his baby daughter. Could she put her past behind her and be Luke's future?

A PERFECT RESULT *by Alison Roberts*

Second of a Trilogy

Although practice manager Toni Marsh loved her job at St David's Medical Centre and its senior partner, Josh Cooper, she realised it was time to leave. Unrequited love was no fun.

On sale 6th October 2000

Available at most branches of WH Smith, Tesco, Martins, Borders, Easons, Volume One/James Thin and most good paperback bookshops

0009/03a

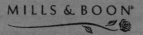

For better, for worse...for ever
Brides and Grooms
Available at branches of WH Smith, Tesco, Martins, Borders, Easons, Volume One/James Thin and most good paperback bookshops

4 BOOKS
AND A SURPRISE GIFT!

We would like to take this opportunity to thank you for reading this Mills & Boon® book by offering you the chance to take FOUR more specially selected titles from the Medical Romance™ series absolutely FREE! We're also making this offer to introduce you to the benefits of the Reader Service™—

★ FREE home delivery   ★ FREE gifts and competitions
★ FREE monthly Newsletter   ★ Exclusive Reader Service discounts
★ Books available before they're in the shops

Accepting these FREE books and gift places you under no obligation to buy; you may cancel at any time, even after receiving your free shipment. Simply complete your details below and return the entire page to the address below. **You don't even need a stamp!**

YES! Please send me 4 free Medical Romance books and a surprise gift. I understand that unless you hear from me, I will receive 6 superb new titles every month for just £2.40 each, postage and packing free. I am under no obligation to purchase any books and may cancel my subscription at any time. The free books and gift will be mine to keep in any case.

M0ZEC

Ms/Mrs/Miss/Mr ....Initials ....
BLOCK CAPITALS PLEASE
Surname ....
Address ....

....

....Postcode ....

Send this whole page to:
UK: FREEPOST CN81, Croydon, CR9 3WZ
EIRE: PO Box 4546, Kilcock, County Kildare (stamp required)